MASTERMINDS

GORDON KORMAN

BALZER + BRAY
An Imprint of HarperCollins*Publishers*

Balzer + Bray is an imprint of HarperCollins Publishers.

Masterminds
Copyright © 2015 by Gordon Korman
All rights reserved. Printed in the United States of America.
No part of this book may be used or reproduced in any manner
whatsoever without written permission except in the case of brief
quotations embodied in critical articles and reviews.
For information address HarperCollins Children's Books, a division of
HarperCollins Publishers, 195 Broadway, New York, NY 10007.
www.harpercollinschildrens.com

Library of Congress Cataloging-in-Publication Data
Korman, Gordon.
    Masterminds / Gordon Korman. — First edition.
        pages   cm
    Summary: "A group of kids discover they were cloned from the DNA
of some of the greatest criminal masterminds in history for a sociological
experiment"— Provided by publisher.
    ISBN 978-0-06-229996-3 (hardback)
    ISBN 978-0-06-239113-1 (int.)
    [1. Cloning—Fiction. 2. Experiments—Fiction. 3. Criminals—
Fiction.] I. Title.
PZ7.K8369Mas   2015   2014026839
[Fic]—dc23   CIP
                                                        AC

15 16 17 18   PC/RRDH   10 9 8 7 6 5 4 3 2
❖
First Edition

For Jay Korman, Sports Mastermind

MASTERMINDS

1

ELI FRIEDEN

It's a one-in-a-million shot, and we nail it.

Just not in the way we planned.

I lie against the cool stone of the pool deck and peer into the filter opening. I can make out the tip of the boomerang, but I can't quite jam my hand in deep enough to get a grip on it. "It's stuck."

"What are the odds?" Randy groans. "You could throw that thing fifty thousand times and never get anywhere near the filter. But one little challenge, and bull's-eye."

Randy's famous around Serenity for his "challenges," which usually involve catching something uncatchable while riding a bicycle, jumping on a pogo stick, swinging on a rope, or rolling inside a truck tire. As his best friend, I'm usually the guinea pig for Randy's cockamamie ideas.

Like today's challenge: Randy throws the boomerang out the window of the tree house and I'm supposed to leap off the diving board, snatch it out of midair, and do a cannonball into the pool. Only I miss, the cannonball turns into more of a belly flop, and the boomerang disappears inside the filter.

"Maybe Mr. Amani can get it out," I suggest. He's the local handyman, whose job includes pool maintenance and just about everything else from plumbing and electrical work to ridding your crawl space of scorpions and baby armadillos.

"And maybe he can't, which means my folks will have to call the pool guys."

That's a much bigger deal than it sounds like. There's no pool company in Serenity, and the nearest town is eighty miles away. It can take weeks to get anybody to schedule a trip out here, and in the meantime your pool turns to soup. Mr. and Mrs. Hardaway aren't going to be thrilled with this—although they're pretty used to it, having dealt with Randy for thirteen years.

It's definitely a drawback to living in a small town in the middle of nowhere. Every time something like this comes up, though, my dad just points to the newspaper clipping on our fridge:

SERENITY VOTED #1 IN USA FOR
STANDARD OF LIVING

He leads me through the bullet points in the article: no crime, no unemployment, no poverty, and no homelessness. The amazing part isn't so much that we have none of those things, but that other towns do, and they're okay with it. It must be awful. Of course, there are only 185 people in Serenity, so it's not so hard to make sure all of them have someplace to live and work. We've got the Serenity Plastics Works, one of the largest producers of orange traffic cones in the United States. Our school has the highest test scores in New Mexico. We're right on the edge of Carson National Forest, surrounded by canyons, foothills, and woods, and the sun shines practically every day. True, it gets pretty hot sometimes, but we don't bake like they do in those real desert towns. No wonder Dad's so proud. He's the mayor, which sounds like a big deal, but it really isn't. His salary as mayor is one dollar per year, and he always claims he's overpaid.

Our parents constantly remind us how lucky we are, and we always roll our eyes. But you know what? They're right. We *are* lucky—just not when the pool filter is busted, and the nearest repair is in Taos.

Randy makes an executive decision. "I'm not going to tell my folks about it. I'll just act ten times as amazed as everybody else when they find the boomerang in there."

I'm a little uncomfortable. That feels like lying. I know people do it all the time on TV and in books. But here, we're honest no matter what. Even when it's hard to be, or when it could get you in trouble. That might sound a little too good to be true, but I think that's why people here are so happy.

"We could go to *my* pool," I suggest, anxious to change the subject. "No boomerang, though." My dad is twenty times as strict as the Hardaways. He's the school principal as well as the mayor. That *is* a big a job. There's only one school in town.

"Nah, I'm sick of swimming."

"We could hang out in the tree house."

"Boring," he declares. "Every kid in town has a tree house and none of them are any fun. And don't say video games either. It doesn't matter how good your home theater is when all your games are lame."

"*Our* games aren't so lame," I remind him. Randy and I have figured out a way to tweak the game software to unlock hidden features, like crashing cars and fighting with real weapons. Turns out I've got a knack for that kind of thing. I can do it with my iPad and computers too. It's strictly hush-hush, because everybody in Serenity is anti-violence. I am, too, but in a video game, I figure where's the harm in it? It's not like it's actually happening.

"Yawn." Randy gets this way sometimes, where nothing satisfies him. Basically, he's a crab. Believe it or not, it's one of the main reasons I like him. You don't hear much complaining in Serenity. Randy always manages to find something, though. It's almost as if he's daring the universe to do a better job, no matter how great things already are. I think my dad would be happier if I found a different best friend. But let's face it, in a town with only thirty kids, there's not much to choose from. And anyway, you don't *find* best friends. Best friends just *happen*.

"So what are we going to do?" I ask him.

"Let's get out of here. Let's *go* somewhere."

I brighten. "They've built that new high slide at the park."

He's unimpressed. "Big deal. You climb up so you can come down. Let's do something *cool*."

"Like what?"

"Like—" His eyes dance. "Check out the most awesome old sports car you've ever seen."

"Sports car?" I echo. When you live in a place this

small, not only do you know every car; you could probably recite the license plate numbers by heart. When somebody gets a new vehicle, three-quarters of the town show up to see it. There are plenty of fancy SUVs and sedans, but no sports cars.

"It was the weirdest thing. My dad and I were hiking a few miles out of town and we found an old, abandoned ranch—busted-up fences and a house that was nothing but a pile of toothpicks. The only thing standing was this rusted Quonset hut. And when we went inside, the car was there. The tires were flat, and the whole thing was buried in dust and spiderwebs, but it was beautiful. My dad said it was Italian—an Alfa Romeo. It had Colorado license plates from 1961."

"Wow," I say.

"Yeah," he enthuses. "Let's go see it."

"What—right now?"

Randy shrugs. "What are you waiting for—Christmas? It's not too far. Grab your bike and let's go."

I hesitate. "I have to ask my dad."

He looks pained. "Bad idea. I know your old man."

Poor Dad. Felix Frieden is kind of a joke among the kids in town, with his three-piece suits, and his shined shoes, and his no-nonsense attitude. They just see his principal side.

Randy has a point, though. "You think he'll say no?"

"Why give him the chance?" Randy insists. "The car's only a few miles away. We'll be there and back before he even knows you're gone. Come on, Eli, live a little."

"It's just—" I'm embarrassed to say it, but I have to be honest. "I've never been out of town."

"Neither have I—not since we visited my grandma when I was six—"

"No," I interrupt. "I've never been *anywhere* out of town. Not even where your dad took you hiking."

"What about that time in science when our class went fossil hunting?" he challenges.

"That was still inside the town limits. Mrs. Laska said so."

He's amazed. "But haven't you ever passed that stupid sign—the one that says: *Now Leaving Serenity—America's Ideal Community*?"

I shake my head. "I've never even seen it."

"Well, you're going to see it today," he decides. "Grab your bike."

That's another thing about Randy. He won't take no

for an answer. He doesn't exactly bring out the best in me, but we have a great time together, and that counts for a lot. He does the things I daydream about but don't have the guts to try.

Until today.

Only one road passes through Serenity, a two-lane paved ribbon everybody calls Old County Six. We pedal west along it, riding right down the center over the faded, broken line. There's little fear of meeting traffic in either direction. All decent highways cross New Mexico well to the south. If you hit Serenity, chances are you're lost.

As we bike on, I spot the gully that was the site of the fossil-hunting trip. I am now farther from home than I've ever been in my life. Can it really be this easy? You just jump on a bicycle and ride out of town? It seems like cheating somehow, breaking some overarching Law of the Way Things Are Supposed to Be. Yet here I am, just doing it. It's kind of exhilarating—at least, I've never been so aware of the beating of my heart and the blood pumping through my veins.

I feel a little strange about not telling Dad. Not that I need his permission—I'm thirteen years old. Besides, he never specifically said *not* to ride my bike out past the town limits. I'm not breaking any rules, but I know he'll be disappointed if he finds out about this. Face it: If I don't need to ask permission for this ride, how come I snuck my bike out of the garage? I try to push the thought from my head as I pedal away.

I glance over my shoulder at Serenity—the perfect rows of immaculate white homes, the swimming pools positioned on the lots like aquamarine postage stamps, the basketball hoops lined up like sentries, all lovingly set down amid the striking southwestern landscape. In this view I find my answer to the nagging question of how a person could spend thirteen years here without ever once setting foot outside the town proper. Why would I need to? When it comes to fun or comfort, we've got it all. We've got the stuff adults want too—a great school and great jobs. We've got the three Essential Qualities of Serenity citizens—honesty, harmony, and contentment. We've heard about the bigger towns and—even worse— cities. They stink of garbage and everything's crumbling, and crime is so bad that nobody can trust anybody else. People spend their time in fear, hunkered down behind locked doors and alarm systems.

At the same time, it's almost startling how *tiny* the town is, even from this distance of barely a mile. If it wasn't for the factory, you wouldn't notice it unless you knew what to look for. I guess that's the Serenity Miracle our parents are always talking about—that so much quality of life can be held in such a small package.

"How much farther?" I call ahead to Randy.

"Probably another twenty minutes."

After a bend in the road, a tall butte obscures the town altogether. It completes the feeling of being out there.

Randy doesn't seem to notice at all. "Look!" he shouts back at me, waving his arm to the right.

It's the sign Randy mentioned—the one about leaving town. In contrast to spotless and impeccable Serenity, it's surprisingly faded and weather-beaten. I squint at the bottom, where the warning *No Gas Next 78 Miles* has been tacked on.

I've done it. I've left town. I survey the rocky hills and scrub pines and brush. I don't know what to call this, but it's not Serenity anymore. After more than thirteen years, I'm officially Somewhere Else. And how does it make me feel?

To be honest, kind of scared. I've never done this before, never lost visual contact with my hometown. By the time I get to see this Alfa Romeo, I'll be so stressed out that I won't even be able to appreciate it. I'm overthinking this whole business to the point where it's making me sick to my stomach.

Well, I'm not turning back. I made it this far, and Randy will never let me hear the end of it if I don't follow through.

But I really *am* sick—and getting sicker. The nausea grows stronger, rising up the back of my throat. There's no way it's just from being nervous. This is something physical. What did I have for lunch today? I can't remember, but whatever it was, it's coming up, and soon. My stomach twists in a paralyzing cramp, and my head hurts too.

"What's with you, Eli?" Randy calls back in annoyance. "Running out of gas already?" His expression changes when he sees me. "Hey, are you okay?"

I've slowed down, although I hardly notice it. Only pure stubbornness keeps my legs pumping. I'm in agony, blinded by the kind of headache that lodges behind the eyes like a glowing coal, pulsating and doubling in intensity. The pain is unimaginable. It's not just a terrible thing; it's the *only* thing.

I'm not even aware of toppling off the bike until my chin strikes the road. Fire erupts on my forearms where they scrape the rough pavement. I see Randy kneeling over me, feel him shaking me, but I'm powerless to respond. I can only focus on one thought:

I'm dying.

What happens next is so shocking, so bizarre, that I'm sure I'm imagining it, delirious with pain. A loud, rhythmic roar swells around Randy and me, and strong winds whip down on us. A dark shadow moves directly overhead, growing larger and larger as it descends. An enormous military-style helicopter settles on the road, its rotor buffeting us with air.

The hatch opens, and out jump six men in identical indigo uniforms and wine-colored berets.

"Purple People Eaters!" Randy breathes.

Through a fog, I can barely make out the distinctive tunics of the Surety, the security force of the Serenity Plastics Works that doubles as the town police. It takes all the strength I have left to spread my arms to the rescuers.

"Help me," I whisper, wondering if they can even hear me over the thunder of the chopper.

"Eli . . ."

I can't seem to pinpoint the source of the voice. Through blurry vision, I can just make out the outline of a face peering down from above.

"Eli, wake up."

"Dad?" I've never been so relieved to see him. My father's familiar features come into focus—thin lips and pale eyes, the color of a frozen lake. It's his Principal Stare, although it's hard to imagine him looking any different if he was an astronaut or a fruit picker or a rock star. Most kids go a long way to avoid that expression, but to me, it's familiar and even comforting, my earliest memory.

I'm in one of the two beds in Serenity's tiny doctor's office and health clinic. An IV tube tugs at my arm. And that means . . .

It's all true. It comes back like a delayed-reaction recollection of a terrible nightmare. The bikes. The collapse. The Purple People Eaters . . .

"I never thought I'd see you again, Dad." The lump in my throat swells to cantaloupe size. "I never thought I'd see anybody!"

The Stare softens and he leans over and hugs me. "You gave us quite a scare."

"What happened?" I feel better, but by no means back to normal. An impenetrable grogginess covers me like a curtain. The nausea and headache are gone, but the memory of so much pain and fear haunt me. The idea that it's possible to feel so awful, and that maybe I'll feel that way again one day—it's changed me.

On the other hand, I'm alive, which is kind of a surprise. "What happened?" I repeat.

Dad breaks the hug. He tries, but he's just not a touchy-feely guy. "Dr. Bruder isn't quite sure. Dehydration, maybe."

"I was fine until suddenly I wasn't anymore. I was on my knees throwing up nothing and holding on to my head to keep it from falling off." My voice cracks a little. "I honestly believed I was going to die."

"But we can't rule out the possibility of an extreme allergic reaction to something growing out there," Dad goes on briskly.

I stare at him, wanting to be babied just a few minutes longer. Briefly I wonder if my mom would have been the warm and fuzzy parent. She died when I was little, so I'll never know. I don't even remember the smiling face in her portrait on our mantel. It's my job to replace the flowers every week. The picture is familiar, but the person in it is a stranger.

Don't get me wrong. My father has always been there for me. I spit up on his tailored suits as a baby. When I toddled my first steps, his sure hands steadied me. I even remember him in the pool supporting my stomach when

I was learning to swim—no small thing for a guy who rarely loosens his tie. But a teddy bear he's not.

"Is Randy all right? Did the Purple People Eaters pick him up too?"

The pale eyes frost over in disapproval. "We don't use that term."

I bite my tongue. *Maybe you don't, but that's what every kid in town calls them. What do you expect when you dress them up like a platoon in plum?*

"You're very lucky the Surety stumbled on you when they did," he continues.

"Stumbled?" It isn't exactly how I'd describe it. "Is that what you'd call a giant helicopter filled with purple storm troopers descending from the sky in a blizzard of flying dust?"

When my father frowns, his lips retreat into a pencil-thin line above his chin. "Storm troopers—where would you pick up a word like that?"

"From school," I reply. "I'm in eighth grade, Dad. We know about armies. We even know they have to fight wars sometimes."

He sighs. "I suppose. We're citizens of the larger world too—not just our own town. I wish that everybody could share the life we have here."

"Tell me about it," I agree. "Hey, Dad, why do the Purple—the Surety have their own helicopter?"

"It belongs to the factory. We're fortunate to have a company like the Plastics Works that looks after us so well. A lot of communities our size don't enjoy our resources."

"Yeah," I persist, "but why do they *need* it here? We're completely safe."

He looks surprised. "Well, they just saved your bacon, didn't they? In a big city, that helicopter might be needed for police surveillance. Here we have the luxury to use it to help people. It's just another thing that makes Serenity such a special place, don't you agree?"

But for once, I'm not sure whether I agree or not, because the memory of the chopper triggers other images: rough hands hauling me aboard the craft; a stifled "Hey!" from Randy, hitting the deck beside me; the sound of the bikes being crammed into the cargo hold; a dizzying take-off, which finally brings up lunch; Serenity viewed from high above, growing steadily larger as we come in for a landing.

Then, pounding feet, a babble of anxious voices. Purple People Eaters, Dr. Bruder, my father, all talking at once.

"Here!"

"Hold the stretcher steady!"

"Quickly!"

"Put him out!"

The needle pierces my arm and I'm fading, but I can hear a response. "Yes, Mr. Hammerstrom."

Hammerstrom?

At that point, the sedative takes effect and everything goes black.

Dad kisses my forehead. That doesn't happen very often, proving how much this incident must have shaken him. "Now get some rest, Eli. Dr. Bruder wants to observe you for a couple of days."

I know I should just be grateful to be alive. But the curiosity is boiling inside me and I can't help it. "What's Hammerstrom?"

He's almost gone, but the question freezes him in the doorway. "I beg your pardon?"

"When they took me out of the helicopter, someone mentioned Hammerstrom."

"One of the Surety goes by that name," Dad replies.

I try not to smile. *Wow, there's a Purple People Eater named Hammerstrom! I've got to tell Randy!*

Although everybody knows everybody in Serenity, that doesn't extend to the Surety. They keep to themselves, which makes them kind of nameless and faceless. You see them around town, but the only time you ever get close is on Serenity Day, for the annual Surety-versus-Plastics-Works tug-of-war. That's also when they do their drill team parade, which looks like someone spilled grape juice on the Grenadier Guards in front of Buckingham Palace.

"Now put it out of your mind," my father continues. "You're safe and it's all over."

It's meant to be soothing, but it sounds a little like an order.

I resist a wild impulse to snap a salute.

2

AMBER LASKA

THINGS TO DO TODAY (UNPRIORITIZED)

- Piano Practice (1.5 hours)
- Ballet Practice (1 hour)
- Math Test Corrections (to bring up grade from 94)
- Meditation (need new mantra–download English-Sanskrit translation app)
- Make Farewell Card for Randy (optional)
- Work on Book with Tori
- Work on Serenity Day Project with Tori
- Sleepover at Tori's (unconfirmed; Tori might sleep over here)

I frown at the list, and then change *optional* to *mandatory*. Maybe Randy's not my favorite person—I think he's a troublemaker. But I feel terrible for anybody who has to move away from Serenity. No other place could ever be as good.

The scene where he breaks the news keeps replaying itself in my head. He's being sent to live with his grandparents in Colorado.

"You mean"—my mind can barely take it in—"you're *leaving* Serenity?"

He nods grimly. "They have a small farm, and they're getting older, so they need some help."

He's devastated. And what about Eli? He's still in the health clinic from that weird accident. I shudder just thinking about it. You're shut away with no visitors, and when you finally get out, the first thing you hear is that your best friend is moving away? I can only imagine what it would be like to lose Tori, who I've seen every single day as long as I can remember.

"Can't your grandparents hire somebody?" Tori asks.

Randy shrugs. "My mom says they can't afford to. It's just a small place."

We stare at him like he's speaking a foreign language. None of us has ever met anybody with money problems.

The plastics factory is always busy, and everyone who wants a job has one. We're not rich in Serenity, but we're all really comfortable. I mean, we know about poor people, but that kind of thing happens in other places. It's the saddest thing I've ever heard—not being able to afford a house or even food to eat.

One time Tori and I saw this movie where a family gets their power shut off because they can't pay their electric bill. It's hard to imagine that situation in Serenity. Maybe you don't pay your water bill so you can't fill up your pool? But here, there's plenty of money to go around, so *everybody* pays their bills. It's just another reason why I'd never leave Serenity—until college, of course. We're too tiny to have our own university—though I wish we did. Even then, I intend to stay as close to home as possible, at the University of New Mexico at Taos. I'm careful to keep my interests and hobbies limited to things you can major in at Taos, like English, music, and dance. That's why I gave up learning Chinese last year. No sense in wasting my time on something that isn't going to go anywhere.

It seems to me that they're ignoring an obvious solution. "Why don't your grandparents sell their farm and come to live here?"

He looks miserable. "It's already decided. I'm going."

"Poor you," laughs Malik Bruder, the doctor's son. "You might actually have some fun in the big bad world out there."

"Can you be serious for once?" I'm so not in the mood for this. "What do you consider fun? Living in a crumbling, dangerous city where people are packed in like sardines?"

Malik smirks at me. He always manages to look like nothing bothers him. "You'd be surprised, Laska."

"And you know *so* much about the world," I shoot back. "With your C-plus average and your interest in—" I pretend to rack my brain. "Oh, right—absolutely nothing!"

He seems amused. "Have you ever been anywhere but here?"

"You haven't either."

"True," he admits. "But the minute I'm old enough, I'm out of here. NYC all the way, baby!" He always calls it by its initials—*en-why-see.*

"Don't say that!" pleads Hector Amani, Malik's number one fan. "It's not like Serenity out there. People take advantage of you!"

Hah. Malik has made an art form out of strong-arming Hector into doing things for him. When it comes to taking advantage, NYC would have a hard time coming up with someone as good as Malik.

Malik shifts his gaze over to Hector. "You're perfect for this place. Me? I'm going to see the world."

"*You can waste your whole life wandering only to find that what you're searching for is right in your own backyard,*" I return. I didn't make that up. That's what it says on the gazebo in Serenity Park. It's kind of the town motto. Tori and I are working on a picture book based on it, called *Your Own Backyard*. My mom is a teacher at the school, and she's going to set it up so we can read it to the lower-grade kids when we're done. If it's any good, naturally.

By this time, Randy looks terrified and I feel guilty. Here we are, talking about how the outside world is unlivable, and that's where he's going. But what can we say? That it's just as good as Serenity? That's another thing outsiders do that we don't. They lie.

Malik notices it too. "Trust me, Randy. You're the lucky one. If the rest of the world is so bad, how come so many people live there? There are, like, seven billion of them, and only 185 of us. Case closed."

Malik is infuriating. But one of the things we learn in school is that anger is the emotion of a lesser person. So I just smile. "You know it doesn't work that way."

"How do you know it doesn't?"

Before I can answer, my mom rings the handbell to call us in for math, which is our first afternoon class except on Tuesdays, when we have science, and Thursdays, when we have Contentment. It's a full schedule when you add in social studies, Meditation, and gym. We're in the middle of the water polo unit now, because Serenity Day is coming up. We always cap off the celebration with the big game. It's my favorite holiday of the year.

I lead the group back into the building. When your mother is the teacher, you have to be just a little better than everybody else. It's a lot of pressure to be the best behaved, the most involved, and to get the highest grades. That's why I make lists of everything I need to do. It helps me stay focused—control is key.

Example: When we reach the classroom, there's always a basket of desserts on the teacher's desk—cookies, cupcakes; today it's donuts. We're supposed to take only one, but it's on the honor system. Mom's still outside, so nobody's watching us.

I'm two pounds off my goal weight, so I don't take any. Tori helps herself to one, like most of the kids. Hector takes a donut, and, when nobody's looking, sneaks another half.

Malik? He inhales about four. He's proud of himself too—standing at the basket, grinning smugly, lips smacking, icing staining his fingers, when Mom comes in for the afternoon. He's practically daring her to call him out.

Malik thinks he's so cool because he breaks rules. But he's not as smart as he thinks he is—especially when it comes to the world outside Serenity. In fact, I know a lot more about it than he does.

It happened a few months ago. Tori and I were in the park working on *Your Own Backyard.* She had to go, but I stayed to practice my pliés, since I was twenty minutes short on ballet that day. Control, remember?

Anyway, I was right by the Serenity Cup, which is this huge silver trophy on permanent display on a pedestal in the center of the park. It's our town's pride and joy, presented by President Roosevelt way back when Serenity was founded in 1937. It sits in a Plexiglas case, and nobody ever walks through the park without checking it out, even though we've all seen it a million times.

So that day, I look at it for time number a million and one, and there's something I've never noticed before—a padlock through a little hasp in the corner of the case.

Then I spot the work crew—two men in heavy boots. One is up a ladder, and the second is holding it steady.

They appear to be snipping branches off an overgrown sycamore tree. Here's the thing, though: they're not from here. Everybody in Serenity knows everybody else, except maybe some of the Purple People Eaters. But I've never seen these guys before.

Sure enough, there's a pickup truck parked by the side of the roadway. *Ray's Tree Service, Taos, New Mexico* is stenciled on the door. I have an astounding thought! Did they lock the case because they're afraid one of these strangers might *steal* the Serenity Cup? We've all heard the horror stories about other places, but this is the first time it's ever crossed my mind that outsiders might bring their dishonest ways here.

Even though I'm nervous, I'm also a little intrigued. Meeting new people doesn't happen very often. There are only 184 possible choices, and I already know almost all of them.

I decide to go over and introduce myself. "Hi, I'm Amber."

One says "Hi" back. The other tells me, "We're working here, kid," not in a mean way, but the way adults sometimes talk when they're too busy to be bothered with you. I guess I look a little wounded, because he adds, "Watch your head. There are branches coming down. I wouldn't want you to get hurt."

"Oh, right. Thanks." I suppose it's nice of him to look out for my safety.

I retreat a few steps toward the truck, and that's when I notice the newspaper on the driver's seat. It's something called *USA Today*. A newspaper for the whole country? People in Serenity read the *Pax*, which is published right here. This paper must be big in Taos, and maybe other places, since it says *USA*.

Suddenly, I'm staring at the headline:

ACTOR'S DEATH RULED MURDER

I turn to the tree guys. "What's murder?"

They stare at me like I'm some exotic cockroach that just crawled up out of the ground. The ladder holder says, "Seriously?"

"I've never seen that word before," I explain. "What does it mean?"

The man in the tree snorts a laugh. "Murder is having to prune branches on a hot day."

"Tell me about it!" his partner chimes in.

I can tell they're laughing at me, and I'm embarrassed although I don't really know why, so I change my tactic.

"Can I have your newspaper?"

"Oh, sure, kid. Knock yourself out. And while you're at it, you'd better get yourself a dictionary."

I reach in the driver's side window, and pick up the *USA Today*. My eyes are drawn back to the lead story:

```
It began as a grisly mystery: blood-
stained walls in a Hollywood hotel
suite; a Browning pistol still clutched
in the victim's limp hand; a famous
face contorted in death . . .
```

"Heads up!"

A leafy branch hits the ground at my feet, and I scramble out of there, calling, "Thanks for the paper." I can feel the newsprint crackling in my hands, almost as if there's an electric current running through it. It's clear to me that I'm holding something powerful and important, although I have no idea how I know this.

When I get home, I hide the *USA Today* in the garage between the spare air-conditioner filters. I'm not sure why I don't show it to my parents, especially my mom. We're really close, since I see her all day at school, and then all night at home. I don't even tell Tori, and we're practically two halves of the same person. I know that keeping secrets is like chiseling at the mortar between bricks in a wall. But this feels different. This is uniquely *mine*. So I have this urge to keep it for myself.

Over the next few days, I read that paper from cover to cover, soaking up every word. Some of the stories are the same as what the *Pax* prints—stuff about the president, and the sports scores. But that's where the similarity ends. Put it this way: I know what murder is now. They also call it *homicide*—another word I never heard before.

Our parents are always reminding us how lucky we are to be spared the kind of problems they have in other places. But that's not the same as seeing it spelled out in black-and-white—reading the descriptions of the crime scenes, hearing about the victims and their poor families, following the police officers who make the arrests, and the court cases where criminals are brought to justice.

And it's not an occasional thing either. I count seven people dying because of murder, just in one *USA Today*! There are even more robberies—and sometimes the murders and the robberies happen together. There are other things we never read about in the *Pax*—things like wars, kidnappings, riots, and acts of terrorism.

Every time I put my *USA Today* back in its hiding

place, my head is spinning with more questions. What kind of people would do such horrible things? There's nobody like that in Serenity. What if murder comes here? Is that why there are so many Purple People Eaters, and why they have their own helicopter—to protect us from all this?

I calm myself down with a little meditation. It's more proof that our parents did the right thing by raising us here, where we're safe.

One thing bothers me, though. Why doesn't the *Pax* print the bad stories that are in *USA Today*? Is it because we don't have to worry about things like murder? Just because we live here doesn't mean we shouldn't know about the outside world. What about someone like poor Randy? When he gets to his grandparents, will he be ready?

I agree that *USA Today* is upsetting, but it feels really honest.

At dinner that night, my mother brings up the subject of Randy moving to Colorado. "How did the kids react?" she asks. "It must be hard to lose a friend you've known for so long."

"Yeah," I agree. "It's murder."

My father drops his fork with a clatter.

Mom stares at me. "Where would you pick up a horrible word like that?"

"From the newspaper."

Dad frowns. "Don't be dishonest, Amber. The *Pax* would never—"

"It wasn't the *Pax*. It was in *USA Today*."

"But how—?" For an instant, my mother's voice rises sharply. Then she catches herself, and when she speaks again, she sounds calm. "I'm a little—surprised that you found an outside newspaper. The *Pax* is all we read around here."

"There were these tree trimmers in the park." It feels good to get it off my chest after so long. "They gave it to me."

"When was this?" my father probes.

"A pretty long time ago."

My parents share a meaningful look. I'm thinking: *Are they mad at me?* I never actually lied, but it's pretty obvious that I didn't go out of my way to tell them about it.

But no. Mom's not angry, just interested. "Well, did you learn anything from it?"

I nod. "I learned how lucky we are to live in Serenity."

THINGS TO DO TODAY (UNPRIORITIZED)

- Piano Practice (1.5 hours)
- Ballet Practice (1 hour)
- Finish Contentment Essay
- Tell Tori about *USA Today*

It's funny—once Mom and Dad know about my newspaper, it seems crazy that I never told Tori about it. What could I have been thinking? It just confirms what we learn in Contentment—that the mind has a way of tricking you into thinking you're doing the right thing when you're not.

The truth is, I was keeping a secret. It's a slippery slope.

Mom's still at school, so Tori and I have the house to ourselves. My father's a honcho at the factory, and he's usually not home until dinner.

"Let's go for a swim," she suggests. "Work on our stamina for the big game."

"Okay, but first I want to show you something cool." I lead the way into the garage and duck behind the shelving unit where we keep the spare filters. One by one, I lift them up.

My *USA Today* is gone.

"Well?" Tori prompts.

Weird—for four months I've kept that paper hidden. And now that I'm finally ready to show it to somebody, it turns out I've lost it. How careless can you get?

"Forget it," I tell her. "Let's put our suits on."

3

MALIK BRUDER

I can't wait to move to NYC when I'm older. I'm going to live on the sixtieth floor of a skyscraper, eat junk food all day long, and, who knows, maybe even get a motorcycle.

The only thing more depressing than living in Happy Valley is having to celebrate it. In school, we all have to work on special projects for Serenity Day, which is the holiday where we commemorate the founding of this wonderful community. Sarcasm intended.

Ever notice that everything around here is Serenity-something? Serenity Park, Serenity Square, Serenity Cup. I should rename my toilet the Serenity Bowl.

Anyway, Serenity Day is a big deal. The entire population turns out, which reminds me of a medium-sized wedding on a TV show. We drink lemonade and eat hot dogs, and listen to speeches about how great our town is, and how lucky we are to live here. The activities would be kind of cool if you were about six—three-legged race, beanbag toss, real prime-time stuff. And Happy Valley is so backward they can't even get that right. Last year, in ring toss, they gave me a set of rings as wide as hula hoops. I was wiping up the competition until Amber started complaining it was unfair. Oh, that Laska. When it comes to fun, she's kind of like Kryptonite.

Whatever. The hot dogs aren't bad.

Happy Valley is so small that the town officials are basically just our parents. Mr. Frieden is the mayor. My mother is the comptroller, in charge of all the finances. Hector's mom is the recording secretary. You get the picture. Not only are the speeches lame, but they're delivered by people who are normally reminding you to floss or take out the garbage.

The highlight of the day is the big water polo match between Team Solidarity and Team Community. Actually, that part's pretty good. Water polo is just about the only chance to take out some of my frustration at living here. I accomplish this by aiming the ball at my opponents' heads. I wouldn't exactly call it textbook strategy, but then again, I wouldn't exactly call Happy Valley a town either.

Believe it or not, people get pretty rah-rah about water polo around here, because the season synchs up with Serenity Day. Nobody gets this excited about our other three sports, badminton, gymnastics, and croquet. But it can be pretty wild at the pool when Community and Solidarity battle it out. Hector's parents always cheer the loudest. I think they're just thrilled that he's made it through another big game without drowning.

Don't get me wrong: I love Hector. Driving Hector crazy is my favorite form of entertainment.

All the dopey chores my parents cook up for me—he does them, no complaints, just to hear me say thanks. I can't say that too often, though. Don't want to spoil the guy.

I haven't had to cut the grass, rake leaves, or pick up some random thing at the store in years. Hector's the ultimate school accessory too. He did a great job on my research paper on tigers—it got a B-plus, which isn't bad for me. Any higher, and Mrs. Laska might get suspicious. Good old Hector.

I guess what I'm saying is he's fun to have around. And fun is hard to come by in Serenity, New Mexico, the most boring pimple on the rocky butt of the Southwest. Not that I have anything to compare it to. I've never been past the city limits. And I use the word *city* very generously.

Wherever I go, I can count on Hector trailing along. Poor kid—when I ride my skateboard, he has to sprint. He sweats a lot. I try not to let him see me laughing.

Then there's the day I look over my shoulder, and the little shrimp's coming around the corner, struggling along on a skateboard of his own. He rides it like he has one leg instead of two. Or maybe it has square wheels. His parents don't seem to like him very much—it's kind of sad. They probably bought him a lousy one.

He looks terrified that he's going to kill himself. The only thing keeping him going is the hope that I'm going to see him and be impressed.

"Malik! Back here!"

I pretend not to hear.

"Hey, wait up!"

It goes on like this for a while. His pleas for attention grow more desperate as he runs out of breath.

Eventually I figure he's had enough, so I stop. The goofy grin on his face as he finally rolls up is totally worth it.

"I got a skateboard!"

So what? We get everything we want in Serenity—

pools, trampolines, video game systems. I remember when we were six, we got those big electric cars. Mine was the Hummer; Hector went for some kind of Mercedes. This, in a community where you can walk from one side to the other in eight minutes, max, even on first-grade legs. We should be the poster town for spoiling your kids. Maybe that's why Contentment is one of our main classes at school. I wonder how they teach Contentment in places where kids don't have as much stuff.

Now he's waiting—dying for me to say something.

So I don't.

He pushes. "What do you think?"

"About what?"

He gets shy. "I figured you could give me some pointers—you know, because you're so good."

That gives me an idea. "Follow me!" With a few pumps of my leg, I'm up to full speed, leading him on an obstacle course through the hardest streets in town—rough road surfaces, speed bumps, sewer gratings. The houses glide by, white and immaculate, not a shutter out of position; the lawns are groomed and green, the flower beds well tended and perfect. Even the pink flamingoes have been freshly power-washed. It's like an insult to manhood.

I glance over my shoulder and feel a twinge of something close to pride. Hector's following—way behind, but give him props, he's following. I've got one more card up my sleeve, and it's the ace of spades. I wheel around the circle onto Fellowship Avenue, which runs past the plastics factory. The thing is Fellowship is the steepest hill in town. It took me years to get up the courage to attempt it on a skateboard. There's no way a newbie like Hector can handle it.

I fly down the grade, grooving on the wind, which is strong enough to cut into the heat of the day. Then I turn and look up. The least I can do is wait at the bottom to pick up the pieces as they land. Hector hesitates, but only for a second. Then he's on the way down, his body straight as a poker, his arms windmilling for balance as the board accelerates. I almost wish he would fall off now, before he picks up enough speed for it to be a total wipeout. My dad's the local doctor, but he doesn't need me to drum up business.

With a click, the factory's long electronic rear gate slides open, and a double-wide flatbed truck begins to nose out into the street. The payload is piled high with orange traffic cones—hundreds of them; maybe thousands. It's a familiar sight around Serenity—a shipment of cones heading out of town.

The truck tries to turn up Fellowship, but it's too long, so the driver has to take another cut. That's when I realize that the whole street is blocked, and there's no way Hector is going to be able to stop a speeding skateboard in time.

"Hector—jump—*jump!*"

Doesn't it figure? All day he's been trying to get me to talk to him. And now he's too petrified to listen—although I probably would be, too, if I was hurtling at terminal velocity toward a giant truck.

I hop off my board and start up the slope, sprinting flat-out. I know a moment of real fear when I see how fast he's coming. But it's too late to think about that now. It's my fault he's on this hill to begin with. I can't let him get killed.

"Jump, idiot!"

He's frozen like a statue.

I slip past the transport before the driver backs up again for the second cut. I line the kid up, and snatch him bodily off his board, which rolls under the truck, and keeps on going. The two of us hit the pavement hard, somersaulting one over the other. We take a pretty big beating, bumping and scraping along the pavement. At one point,

I see that my shirt is covered in blood, and I kind of panic before I realize that it's coming from Hector's nose.

The driver jumps out of the truck and comes over to see if we're still alive. "Are you okay? Don't you know it's dangerous to skateboard down a hill like that?"

The guy seems to think that *I* was the one who almost got killed, since I've got the most blood on me. But Hector looks pretty bad, too, and his nose is still gushing. He struggles to his feet, steadying himself against the side of the truck and bleeding all over a stack of cones. Three big sneezes spray gore over a wide area.

The driver is worried. "Maybe I should call the Surety."

That's all we have to hear. We're right by the factory, so there must be Purple People Eaters just on the other side of the gate. Those guys creep me out. And who knows the penalty for bleeding on their precious traffic cones?

"It's okay, mister," Hector sniffles. "We're fine."

Well, what do you know? Shrimp has the brains to be cool about something. We both get up, sidestep the truck, and run after our skateboards.

At the bottom of the slope, we pick up our boards and walk. Hector is impressed. "Do you believe that? We bled together! Like blood brothers!"

I have to laugh. "If you don't shut up, I'm going to take you back to the top of the hill." His nose twitches. "And don't sneeze on me! You want me to get sick?"

"I don't have a cold. Didn't you see how dusty those cones were? I'm allergic."

"Being a wimp doesn't count as an allergy."

I learn two things that day. First, never skateboard with Hector Amani. I mean, I love messing with the kid and all that. But he's such a spaz that he's going to get himself killed one of these days, and I don't want that to be on me.

Second, the Serenity Plastics Works is about as intelligently run as everything else in this one-horse town. Whenever I see one of those trucks now, I check it out. Hector's right—those cones really *are* covered in dust. Who knows how long their product sits around before they bother to ship it out?

This is the factory that's supposed to be our claim to fame? Those cones aren't just dusty; they're dirty. On one of the trucks, there's this dark, crusty stuff on some of them. If I didn't know better, I'd swear it's Hector's nosebleed.

But all that happened days ago.

4

ELI FRIEDEN

There's something different about Randy, and it isn't just because he's leaving.

He never comes to see me in the clinic, even though I'm there two nights.

"I knew you were okay," is his shrugged explanation when I finally get over to his house. "What's the point of us hanging around a hospital bed, listening to Bruder's lame jokes?"

If it happened to you, I'd be there in a heartbeat! I almost blurt.

I'm sort of hurt. When Randy broke his ankle last year, I spent even more time than usual at the Hardaways' because I felt bad for him being all cooped up. We even invented a new challenge—crutch-ball home run derby.

That's always been the best part of being best friends with Randy. You spend 80 percent of your time laughing. He can make a game out of anything. I had visions of us racing up and down the hall—me on the wheeled IV stand and him on a rolling instrument cart. Or something even crazier. There's no limit to the guy's creativity.

But now he doesn't even meet my eyes. "I have to pack."

"I'll help," I offer.

No good. "My mom's driving me nuts with it. She's got everything in these color-coded boxes. It's a train wreck up there."

"I still don't understand why you have to go at all."

"Yeah, tell me about it."

I can tell I've hit a nerve, so I try to cheer him up. "Well, we should definitely get in a couple of challenges before you leave. How about the truck-tire scooter jump? We never quite nailed that one."

Just for a moment, the old Randy shows up. His eyes dance. "It occurred to me to stick the boomerang back in the pool filter for old times' sake. I wouldn't even be here to get in trouble for it."

I sigh. "At least you'll be with your grandparents."

He looks at me as if I have a cabbage for a head.

"Randy, did you remember to pack your—" Mrs. Hardaway comes up behind her son and fixes me with an unreadable expression. Anger? Resentment? Fear, even? I'm taken aback. It isn't my fault her parents need help on their farm. That's what's sending Randy away, not me.

Then she stuns me even more. "Sorry, Eli, but Randy has a lot of things to do before he's ready."

In other words, get lost.

My best friend is being shipped off to Colorado, and I'm barely going to have the chance to say good-bye.

We throw Randy a going away party at school, with a frozen yogurt cake and his favorite chips—fiery jalapeño and lime. There are only thirty kids in the whole town— nineteen of us in the upper school classroom, so it isn't exactly a big blowout.

"One of the unique things about Serenity is that we're all like a family," Dad says in his capacity as principal. He chuckles. "There are some extended families larger than our entire population. But when one of our own moves on, it's like we're losing a brother or a nephew. It leaves an empty space that's impossible to fill. We'll miss you, Randy."

I find myself suddenly annoyed. In the past, Dad

has mentioned at least fifty times how much he wished there was another school in town so Randy could go to it. Dad's not going to come close to missing Randy. Isn't that almost like lying?

Mrs. Laska speaks next, but she says some nice things you can tell she really means. At the end, she gives Randy a big hug and actually tears up a little.

"Speech!" calls Stanley Cole, and a few others join in.

Randy's face is bright red. "Who says I like jalapeño chips?"

Even Dad smiles at that one.

Tori Pritel sits down beside me. "I've never seen Randy so embarrassed."

"You can't embarrass Randy. Remember the time he ran out of bathing suits so he played water polo in boxers?" I study the floor. "Then again, what do I know?"

She turns in surprise, her long dark hair shifting on her shoulders. "You should know more than anybody. You guys are best friends."

"You'd think so, right?" I should probably keep my mouth shut, but there's something about Tori that puts me at ease. With Amber, you always feel like you're being judged; with Malik, you're afraid he'll make fun of you, or worse, file it away so he can use it against you later. Tori's the opposite. "Every time I go over to Randy's, it's the same story: 'I have to pack.' How much packing can anybody do? Lewis and Clark didn't pack this much. He's avoiding me."

"He's sad, you're sad," she contends. "Nobody ever leaves town, so we're extra sensitive to any change. Remember how weird it was when Mrs. Delaney got here?"

Mrs. Delaney is our water polo coach. She's super-nice and also a great source of information about the outside world. She came to town about six months ago when she married one of the Purple People Eaters.

"Maybe," I concede, "but that doesn't explain everything. Like why all this is happening so fast. I've barely heard Randy even mention his grandparents before— have you? I'm in the clinic for *two days* and suddenly he's going to *live* with them?"

"I'm guessing the Hardaways have been considering this for a long time," Tori reasons. "They just didn't tell Randy because they didn't want to worry him—you know how parents are. So when the decision gets made, it seems like it's coming out of nowhere. But it's really been brewing awhile."

Tori doesn't get great grades in school, but she's really smart in a common sense way. Not that it helps me feel any better. Nothing will—except Randy announcing that he isn't moving after all.

The party fizzles. Randy has no appetite, which saddles us with a lot of uneaten chips.

Dad has a solution. "You can each have one more bag. We trust you not to take more than your fair share." He escorts Mrs. Laska out of the room.

Amber scowls at Malik, who already has a huge armload. "We're on the honor system!"

Malik stuffs a fistful into his mouth. "Guess that makes me the most honorable guy in town."

I look over at Randy. His expression never changes.

The next day is Saturday—departure day—although in my mind, Randy's already gone. I'm done banging my head against the wall. Numbness has begun to set in.

Still, I get up early to watch them load the car, which doesn't even appear so full after all that packing. In a way, everything seems totally normal. The Hardaways are going for a drive, something they do occasionally. The only difference is that, this time, when they come back, Randy won't be with them.

He looks pale, and there's no life in his eyes. His parents seem none too happy themselves, and his little sister is crying. I'm trying to swallow a lump in my throat the size of a bowling ball.

It's so awkward. There's no hugging or handshakes. Instead, I give him a piece of paper with my email address on it. "In case you forget." He probably never knew it. We live a grand total of a hundred yards away from each other.

Correction: we used to.

"Let's go, Randy," his father announces. "It's getting late."

They get in the car. He hasn't even said good-bye. The car pulls away from the curb.

Suddenly, he rolls his window down. "I'll write."

I point to the paper in his fist. "Don't lose my email address."

"I'll write," he repeats as if it's the most urgent thing in the world, and I was too stupid to understand the first time. "Think of it as our newest challenge."

Like a few messages back and forth can replace nearly fourteen years of friendship.

As the car makes the turn onto Old County Six, I wave. I couldn't have said anything if I wanted to.

* * *

Now that Randy's gone, it's like the counter on my whole life has been reset. Everything is measured by the moment the Hardaways' car disappeared. There's the first night without Randy; the first weekend without Randy. I can't remember the last time I walked to school alone. It's less than a quarter mile, but it feels longer without the company, the shared yawns and jokes about Purple People Eaters driving by in their pickups. The rapid-fire plop of a fistful of cottonwood seeds splashing into somebody's pool isn't nearly as satisfying when there's no one to hear it with you.

When you spend thirteen years with the same two-and-a-half-dozen kids, losing somebody is like cutting off a finger. Especially when it's your best friend.

At lunch, Amber and Tori are eating together, and Malik, Hector, and Stanley are at one of the picnic tables. Just beyond them are Melanie Brandt and the Fowler twins.

It's probably been like this for years, but I never noticed because I was always paired up myself.

After school comes the first water polo practice without Randy. The pool feels empty somehow, which makes no sense because the same number of us are in the water at any given time.

I'm not the only one missing Randy. He was Team Community's best player.

Mrs. Delaney makes me his replacement, which means I have to go up against Malik, who plays the game like a great white shark with elbows. If you want to be on the winning side on Serenity Day this year, root for Solidarity.

Everyone's already in the locker rooms. I linger poolside, dripping on the towel in my lap. I can't seem to work up the enthusiasm to wrap it around me. Randy and I always used to race a couple of lengths after practice. I'm not about to do it alone, but old habits die hard.

I'm aware of a shifting of weight on the bench and I see that Mrs. Delaney has sat down beside me. "This must be hard for you," she says sympathetically.

I nod. "Malik's really good. Strong."

"And when he can't score on you, he just aims the ball at your face." I guess I look surprised, because she grins. "You think I miss that? I played in college, you know. Division One."

Two things about Mrs. Delaney: she's a lot younger than most of the parents in town, so she remembers what it's like to be a kid. And she's new, so the way things are done in Serenity isn't the whole world to her.

"But that's not what I meant," she goes on. "You must be missing Randy."

"Does it show?"

"Not really," she says. It's a lie, but she's doing it to be nice. "You know, in most places, people pick up and move constantly. It's the normal thing to do. I lost friends that way half a dozen times—either their families moved or mine did. You get used to it."

"Not here you don't."

"True," she admits. "Of course, Serenity's not so easy to get used to either. I'm from Philadelphia, so I never dreamed I'd live in such an isolated place. But then I married Bryan, so I found a way."

Bryan. It amazes me every time I hear it. *There's a Purple People Eater named Bryan. Just like they're human or something.* For the millionth time I think of Randy.

It's hard enough to imagine your teacher having a life outside of school. Throw one of the Surety into the mix, and it's really through the looking glass. Mrs. Delaney once told the class that she met her husband on vacation in Cancún. I'll never shake the picture of this beautiful beach with people swimming and sunbathing, and in the middle of everything there's this Purple People Eater in full-dress uniform, complete with boots and beret. Maybe he double-parked his helicopter by the tiki bar.

I have to ask. "What are the Surety guys like when they're not on duty?"

She gives me a mischievous grin, which makes her appear even younger. "That's classified, mister."

"Classified?"

"You know," she explains, "like government secrets." She stares at me, puzzled that I don't understand.

"It's not honest to keep secrets," I say.

"Sometimes things have to be kept from us for our own good. Like national security. If the president told everybody his plan for that, he'd also be telling the enemy."

I'm even more confused. "Who's the enemy?"

She looks flustered. "Well, there isn't one now. I'm just explaining why certain information has to be classified." She manages to regain her composure a little. "Like your teacher's private life, for example. Your need for honesty stops at my front door."

I can feel my face burning red. "Sorry." But I'm more confused than embarrassed. Dad says the need for honesty *never* stops. I stand up. "I should go change." I start for the locker room.

"I can tell you one thing about the Surety," she calls after me.

I turn around.

"They know you kids call them Purple People Eaters. I think they kind of like it."

5

HECTOR AMANI

I know what everybody says: Malik's not really my friend. He's using me so I'll help him with his homework.

I don't care. They don't know the real Malik. They don't see how he treats me when nobody's looking. Like the time I skateboarded into the truck from the Plastics Works. I said I was fine, but Malik dragged me to the doctor's office so his dad could check out my nose. Malik cares about me, and that's more than I can say about a lot of the people who warn me against him.

Or when I got in trouble for losing my dad's favorite toilet snake, and I couldn't watch TV for three months, Malik let me come over to his house to watch *I Love Lucy*, even though he hates *I Love Lucy*. He only punched me twice, and even those times were because I laughed too loud at the funny parts.

We seem really different, but the truth is, Malik and I have a ton in common. Neither of us has brothers or sisters, and our dads don't work in the plastics factory, which is pretty rare for around here. We're not ordinary size—Malik's the biggest kid in town, and I'm small for my age. We both love hot dogs, although he can eat three to my one.

The main similarity between Malik and me is we don't love Serenity that much, and everybody else thinks it's the best place on earth. Malik doesn't hide the fact that, as soon as he's old enough, he's leaving. We *all* have to leave if we want to go to college—there's no university in Serenity. But I assume what he means is that once he's gone, he's never coming back. Strange that a guy who relies on 24/7 room service from his mom is so anxious to get away. Maybe he expects Mrs. Bruder to come to NYC with him to cook his food and look after his laundry. She might even do it—she's that kind of mother. He complains that she smothers him, but he also complains when the chip bowl gets low. That's how their relationship works. She's constantly nagging; he's constantly yelling, yet they're closer than close. There's this word I heard once: *codependent.* I'm not sure if it comes under honesty, harmony, contentment, or a little of all three.

I don't say anything, but when moving day comes, I'm going to beg Malik to take me with him—to college and beyond. I don't want to stay in this town forever, even though the outside world scares me. It's just too different and unknown.

Until that day, though, we're stuck here, and we're best friends, whether anyone believes it or not. He's my partner for the Serenity Day project. We're making amazing progress, and it's probably going to go even faster once Malik starts helping. It was his idea to build a scale model of Serenity Park using Legos and the crate that the Bruders' new pool table came in. I've been spending all my spare time in the park, mapping and measuring, to make sure we get it exactly right. Malik doesn't get good grades, so most people don't realize what a perfectionist he is. He understands all the schoolwork he gets out of doing. If he tried, he'd probably be the third-best student in town, after Amber and me.

Then again, if Malik was a good student, what would he need me for?

Yesterday, I'm in the park, measuring the display case for the Serenity Cup and hoping it matches the dimensions of the clear plastic Tic Tac container we're using for our project when I spy Stanley Cole and his family. They're picnicking on the lawn by Serenity Square—Stanley, his parents, his kid brother, and their dog, Ortiz. I watch from a distance, but they don't notice me. They're too wrapped up in each other. It kind of makes me uncomfortable. They laugh a lot, like everything's hilarious to them. The dad drops a sandwich and the dog eats it. Hilarious! Stanley wipes out on an exposed tree root. Hilarious! The little kid buries his trucks in the sand, and then cries because he can't find them. Hilarious! Even cleaning up after the dog is a fun family activity. What's the matter with these people? I can't understand why they seem to think that everything in the world has been put there for their amusement.

I can just picture *my* father throwing a Frisbee, or giving me a piggyback ride. Or my mother picking up dog poop—and liking it! It would never happen. Not in this life. When I was eight, I asked my parents for a puppy. They said no, the dog food would be too expensive. I even offered to eat less to save money. No dice. I'm too skinny as it is; it'll stunt my growth. Looking back on it, we live in just as nice a house as anybody in town; we have the same cars and pools and grand pianos. If the Coles can afford dog food, why can't we?

My mom is an executive at the plastics factory, and my dad is the only handyman for eighty miles. If something breaks, it's him or nobody. I know how people look at my parents when we go out. You can feel the respect. They would never waste time having a picnic in the park, or laughing like hyenas about nothing. You won't catch them with their arms around each other. And I can assure you that I've never had a piggyback ride in my life.

Honestly, I don't know how Stanley lives with the humiliation. I see his face, laughing, smiling, grinning, and I know for certain that I never looked like that.

I wonder what it feels like.

"Losers," is Malik's opinion when he finally arrives. "And the biggest loser is you for spying on these idiots when you should be working."

"Poor Stanley," I say. "His parents treat him like he's two years old."

"You don't pick your parents," he tells me. "You get what you get."

I'm surprised. "Your folks are the best!"

He makes a face. "If you like bad jokes and chicken soup."

"I love your mom's chicken soup! And your dad's jokes—" How can I describe it? Dr. Bruder's humor may be corny, but it's comfortable, like an old shirt you don't want to throw out. "Well, I love your mom's chicken soup. Seriously, I wish I had your parents." I'm surprised I said that out loud.

Malik takes it in stride. "You got a roof over your head, same as everybody else. Not that your mother feeds you very much."

"She feeds me plenty. I just don't grow. It isn't anybody's fault."

"Relax," he advises me. "I'm pulling your chain. Your folks are fine. How good can parents be, anyway? It's not like cars, where you can be a Kia or a Bugatti. They're parents."

What he's trying *not* to say is what everybody else in town thinks—that Mom and Dad are bad parents, or at least that they love me less than all the other parents love their kids.

But that's just wrong.

Maybe my folks don't show it, like Malik's mom, or the Pritels, or even Mr. Frieden, who's super-strict because Eli is his whole life. But my parents care about me, and I can prove it.

It's one of my earliest memories—I must have been three or four. I was playing in the sandbox in our backyard. When you're little, you get a swing set and a sandbox before you graduate to the usual tree house and basketball half-court.

I'm making roads with a toy shovel. Serenity is one of the few places where a little kid can re-create the entire street grid in a sandbox.

When I hear the rattling sound, I don't know what it is. I've never heard it before. I turn and come face-to-face with a coiled snake—a diamondback, its tail in the air, poised and ready to strike.

I remember my father flying across the yard. His feet must touch the grass, but to me, he'll always be flying. He reaches out for me but pulls up suddenly as the rattler strikes. The triangular head slices toward me, and then pauses in midair partway between Dad and me. Almost like the snake can't figure out which of us to bite.

It's probably just a second but it feels like forever that the three of us are frozen in time—my father, the rattler, and me. We're silent—even the diamondback has stopped rattling—although Mom is screaming loud enough for all of us.

The snake has had enough. It dashes off, and Dad scoops me up in his arms. It's over that fast. By the time my younger self begins to cry, everything is back to normal, and there's nothing to cry about. I might have forgotten the whole thing except for the conversation I overhear when I'm in bed that night:

"Why did you hesitate?" my mother demands. "He weighs forty pounds, Peter! A snakebite would have killed him for sure!"

"It was a diamondback, Tina," is my father's response. "A little one, too—you know the venom is more concentrated in the very young! What was I supposed to do—get bitten myself?"

"If necessary," Mom replies readily. "You know how valuable he is."

I hear Dad sigh. "You're right. I'm sorry."

Valuable. When they yell at me, or roll their eyes at me; when they ground me for some minor thing that isn't even my fault, I remember that word and hang on to it. When I see another family having fun in a way we never do, I picture how Mom's lips must have moved to form those precious syllables.

I'm *valuable.*

If that's not love, what is it?

6

TORI PRITEL

The Purple People Eaters aren't really purple. Their uniforms are more like a deep blue-violet. Look closely and you'll see it too.

I notice things other people miss. I think it's because I'm an artist, so I have an eye for detail. You know the smokestacks at the Plastics Works? You never see any smoke coming out of them. My parents say it's because the factory is a green industry that doesn't pollute. Steve (aka Dad) says they switched over in 1978. We're ahead of our time in Serenity.

It's important because Amber and I are doing a mural for our Serenity Day project. If there's anything coming out of the chimneys, it would be wrong. We want this to be as authentic as possible. I hope it goes better than the book we were writing together. She says my pictures don't match her story, when it's *obvious* her story doesn't match my pictures. We got into a pretty big argument about that for about fifteen or twenty minutes, until this song we both like came on the radio. Amber and I fight a lot, but twenty minutes is kind of our maximum. She claims I'm immature because, at thirteen, she's technically a teenager and I'm still twelve. She's really only seven months older than me, but she never fails to make a big deal out of it. She says I'm too sensitive, but I'm obviously not. (She also says I use the word *obvious* too much. She might be right about that one.)

I have an artist's studio in our attic. Dad set it up for me. There's a window with a great view of the whole town and Carson National Forest in the background. At dusk, the light on the distant mountain faces reminds me of glowing amethyst.

Come to think of it, the Purples' uniforms have some of that too. Dark amethyst. Is that a real color? (Is there such a thing as *light* amethyst? I'll have to check.)

In the foreground we've decided to draw a cross section of our citizens. Obviously, we can't pose everybody, so we're collecting photographs to use as models. It's pretty interesting to look at still pictures of people you see on a daily basis. Mr. Amani, who's more than a foot taller than his wife; Dr. Bruder with his goofy bow ties; Kurt Osterwald's bright red hair, which is a perfect match for his dad's. Then there's Eli, who's as dark as his father is fair. I'll bet his mom's hair was jet-black. Not that I'm anyone to talk. I look nothing like either of my parents. My dad insists that he found me on eBay. He's joking, obviously. He calls me Torific and I call him Steve.

"I think it would be more appropriate for my twelve-year-old daughter to address me as Dad," he tells me.

"Sure, Steve, I'll get right on that."

He isn't mad. I'm the princess of his heart. Maybe I'm a little old to be called that, but as long as Malik doesn't find out, I figure there's no harm.

Mom and Steve met in the bleachers at a water polo match at the University of Alabama. It was love at first sight. They moved to Serenity because they never wanted to be apart, and the Plastics Works had jobs for both of them. That was important, because they both had student loans to pay back. I always ask them to tell me the story again because it's so romantic. I like to picture them walking hand in hand through the entrance to the plant on their first day of work—not just husband and wife, but coworkers too. (This takes some imagination since the factory grounds are off-limits to nonemployees.)

"Best decision we ever made," Dad says, "because it brought you into our lives."

"You would have had me no matter where you guys lived," I always point out.

He shakes his head. "Wouldn't have been the same. There's something special about this place. You wouldn't have been your Torific self anywhere else."

Steve and I don't see eye to eye on everything. It's my dream to travel to places like New York and even Europe to visit the amazing art museums there. He thinks it's just as good to look at paintings and sculptures on the internet.

It's so obviously not the same. "Come on," I wheedle. "Let's take a trip. When's the last time you and Mom went on vacation? I've never even been outside Serenity."

"We have everything we need right here."

"If I'm going to be an artist," I persist, "I have to learn from the great masters. You can't do that squinting at a screen. I have to walk on the same cobblestones as Michelangelo and Leonardo da Vinci!"

The next time I open up the computer, I find a virtual tour of the Uffizi Gallery in Florence, Italy.

"Steve!" I'm exasperated, but I'm laughing too. His stubbornness is part of what makes him my dad. It's annoying, but deep down I realize I'm pretty lucky with the life I've got.

"I won't be twelve forever, you know," I tell him with a mischievous grin. "I'm going to Europe—if you and Mom won't take me, then I'll go when I'm in college. You guys can't control what I do forever."

That makes him look really uncomfortable. I guess it's hard for any father to deal with the fact that his little girl is growing up.

Later that night, I notice Eli outside my window on Harmony Street. This isn't a huge coincidence. In Serenity, you always see someone you know because you know everybody (except the Purple People Eaters, obviously).

Anyway, there's Eli, walking up and down, looking kind of unsure of himself. I realize that the house he's staring at is Randy's—at least, where Randy used to live before he got sent to his grandparents. What a crummy piece of luck that was. Everybody feels bad about it, but that obviously goes double for Eli.

I abandon my mural and run down to join him on the darkened street. He looks a little embarrassed when I get there, like he's been caught doing something he shouldn't.

"Have you heard anything from Randy?" I ask,

because it's obvious that something's bugging him.

He shakes his head. "It's been two weeks. It's like he's dropped off the face of the earth."

I frown. "What do the Hardaways say?"

"Just that he's really busy and I'll hear from him one of these days."

"That's doesn't make a lot of sense to me," I muse. "How long does it take to shoot an email—*Arrived in Colorado. Everything good?*"

"He told me he'd write. It was the last thing he said before the car drove away."

"He was probably really stressed that day," I reason.

"Yeah, but he said it twice. He made a really big deal out of it." He looks determined. "So I keep asking myself: Why would my best friend promise to write, put such a fine point on it, and then not do it?"

I wish I could help him somehow, or at least wrap my arms around him and tell him everything is going to be okay. (Ha—can you imagine if Malik found out about *that?*) But all I can manage is a shrug.

Eli answers his own question. "I think he did write. I think he wrote before he even left. There's a message for me here somewhere."

There are about a million things wrong with that

logic. For example, if Randy already knew what he wanted to say before he left, why didn't he just say it? What could be so secret? We don't keep secrets here.

But I just say, "A message? Where?"

He doesn't answer, but he's looking past the house into the Hardaways' backyard. "I don't know," he says finally, "but it must be someplace he thinks I'll find it."

I follow his gaze directly to the tree house.

"No problem, then," I say. "I'm sure Mr. and Mrs. Hardaway won't mind if you look around."

"I think the Hardaways are mad at me. It's really weird. They don't talk to me anymore. It's like they talk through me. And when I come around, they make excuses that they have to leave." He sizes me up, as if wondering whether or not he can trust me. "Besides, if Randy left me a hidden message, it was so his parents wouldn't see it."

Now I'm uncomfortable. "So you're—"

"Going to check the tree house." He smiles sheepishly. "At least, I'm trying to work up the guts to."

"I'll go with you," I blurt, surprising even myself. Maybe it's wrong, but there's something intriguing, even irresistible, in the idea of this message from Randy to Eli (if it exists). What could this special forbidden information possibly be? I can't imagine keeping a secret from anyone, much less Amber, *my* best friend. It's almost as if seeing it will open a hidden door I never even knew existed.

"Randy kept an old coffee can in his tree house," Eli confides in me. "When we were little kids, it was kind of his treasure box. He had a rodent skull, and this rock he was convinced was a rare fossil. There was a shark's tooth I'm pretty sure was plastic. We haven't looked at it lately, but I know the can is still there."

"And that's where the message is?" I ask dubiously.

"I don't know. Probably not. Maybe there *is* no message. I have to try, though. But I don't want Randy's parents to see me."

I understand his problem right away. The houses in Serenity have big windows and open rooms. We've got nothing to hide (at least I thought we didn't). Even from here, we can see the flickering of the Hardaways' wide-screen TV. For us to enter the backyard, we'd be parading ourselves right by Mr. and Mrs. Hardaway.

And then it comes to me. I can picture the layout of things from all perspectives. Obviously, it's connected to being an artist, but it's more than that. I understand how things work—like I can envision the finished puzzle before anybody puts the pieces together. It's not anything I do; I just *know*.

So I place myself on the couch with the Hardaways, and design a route that will take us to the tree house without being noticed. We creep along the outside of the fence, and then climb over into the Hardaways' yard once we're under cover of the pool heater. From there, we're up the ladder and into the tree house in short order.

Eli's brought a small flashlight. He finds the coffee can right away. It's nestled in a hole in the tree trunk. With trembling hands, he lifts the lid and dumps the contents of the can out onto the wooden floor.

There they are: the rodent skull, the plastic shark's tooth, and a few other random items that someone a lot younger than us might have considered treasure. There's a stack of three-by-five index cards held together with a rubber band. I take a look at the top one and frown in confusion. There's somebody's photograph at the top and scribbled notes underneath. The face in the picture seems kind of familiar.

"Isn't that—?"

Eli snatches the pack away. "You're not supposed to see these."

But I've already identified the photograph. "That's a Purple People Eater!"

Even in the gloom of the tree house, I can see his face

is red as a tomato. "They're Purple People Eater cards," he confesses in a voice so low it's like he's hoping I won't hear it. "Randy and I made them. You know, kind of like baseball cards, only with—"

"I get it," I assure him, holding out my hand. Reluctantly, he gives me the deck.

I riffle through it. There must be two dozen cards, each one with a photo of a Surety agent (candid, obviously. Purples never pose. These must have been taken on a cell phone from behind hedges or around corners). The facts below are very much like what you'd find on sports cards, with the difference that they're all made up, including the names— RUMP L. STILTSKIN, MIKE "ARACHNOPHOBIA" JONES, ALEXANDER THE GRAPE, SCREAMING MIMI, SECRET AGENT MAN, and even a couple of military titles, MAJOR NOSEHAIR and GENERAL CONFUSION. The "information" looks like real statistics, but it's all crazy stuff, like winning pancake-eating contests and being twelfth in line to the Sultanate of Altoiletstan.

BARON VLADIMIR VON HORSETEETH
Born: 0.003 seconds after the Big Bang
Hobbies: Tearing heads off live chickens,
    flatulence, knitting

Goal: To win Kentucky Derby

Major Accomplishment: Flossing

Favorite Foods: Hay, carrots, sugar cubes

Favorite Color: Thursday

I'm sort of shocked at first. At home and at school, we're taught to practically worship the Surety for the job they do protecting our town. But after a few seconds, I feel the corners of my mouth curling upward. The cards are just—funny. And they fit some of the subjects so well, like Bigfoot, who must wear size eighteen shoes; or Mr. Universe, whose muscles bulge clear through the fabric of his purple tunic; or Sunshine, whose sour-pickle face is the exact opposite of his name. I must have passed Baron Vladimir von Horseteeth dozens of times and noticed those choppers the size of piano keys.

"These are amazing," I tell him. "What gave you the idea to make cards?"

"It was all Randy. We passed one of them and Randy blurted out a nickname for the guy. We were laughing so hard that we kept going, dreaming up all these details. Then we decided to do the cards, so we ran around taking their pictures and brainstorming goofy stuff about them. . . ." He trails off, probably thinking about the great times he and Randy used to have.

I flip another card.

BRYAN

Hobbies: Marrying Mrs. Delaney

Favorite Quote: "Hey, Mrs. Delaney, will you
   marry me?"

"We never came up with much for Bryan," he says apologetically. "Once they're real people, they're not that funny anymore. I wonder which one is Hammerstrom."

"Hammerstrom?"

"Another one of the Purples," he supplies. "Those are the only two names we have—Bryan Delaney and Somebody Hammerstrom."

I replace the rubber band on the card pack. "The other kids have to see these, Eli. They're too good to keep hidden."

He'd probably say no, but he's distracted by the search for this phantom message from Randy. I stick the pack in my pocket as he continues to riffle through the contents of the can again and again. There's no note.

His disappointment is so clear that it almost has a heat signature. It's like losing his best friend all over again.

I'm disappointed, too, but I'm also relieved. Although we're not technically breaking any rules, sneaking around doesn't feel very honest.

"You know, people promise to write all the time," I offer. "They get busy or they forget. It's nothing personal. You're talking about a guy who spends hours making Purple People Eater cards while he's flunking math."

"Sure." He sits back against the wall of the tree house, utterly defeated. Poor Eli. He takes everything so seriously. It's one of the things I like about him, but he can be very hard on himself sometimes.

I shift my weight, and suddenly I'm sitting on a sharp-edged object that makes me jump. I pull it out from under me. It's a wooden boomerang, of all things.

Eli laughs. "Remember Randy's challenges? Well, the latest one . . ." He frowns, a look of discovery coming over his face. *"Think of it as our newest challenge . . ."*

"Huh?"

He's out of the tree house and starting down the ladder before I can ask him where he's going.

I follow, whispering, "Careful!" I can see what he can't—that he's back in view of the Hardaways' couch. At least he's got the brains to keep low. I duck behind a deck chair as he leans over the edge of the pool and reaches into the filter. He digs around for a few seconds, his arm in the opening up to his shoulder. I catch a glimpse of his prize in the moonlight—a white envelope inside three layers of Ziploc bags. It's dripping on the outside, but it looks like the letter is dry.

Eli moves to open the Ziplocs, and I stop him. "Not here!" I hiss.

We retrace our steps to the fence, and retreat the way we came in. Huddled together so close we can feel each other's pounding heartbeats, we peel away the layers of plastic bags and examine the envelope. *ELI* is written on it.

"Randy's handwriting," he says breathlessly. He tears it open, and we begin to read.

> *Eli—*
>
> *I'm not going to live with my grandparents. I'm being sent away to boarding school at McNally Academy in Pueblo, Colorado. I think it's because of what happened when we went out on our bikes that day. I can't explain how, but I get the feeling that some of the kids in Serenity—including you—are special, and I'm not. Nobody will say why, but somehow that bike*

*trip was okay for me but not for you. I'm positive
the answer lies in why you got sick and I didn't.
Maybe the special people can figure it out. I sure
can't.*

*Since you're reading this, you were smart
enough to follow the clues. Thanks for that. I'm
not allowed to contact you, so I guess this is the
only good-bye we're ever going to have. Protect
yourself, Eli. There's something screwy going on
in that town.*

Randy

I stare at the tri-folded paper. "This is nuts!"

Eli's white-faced. "There's nothing special about me."

"Wait a minute—you're taking this seriously?"

He's floundering. "Randy thinks there's a connection
between being special and getting sick . . ."

"Randy's not thinking!" I explode. "He's reacting!
He's angry because he had to move away from his family
and leave the best place in the world to live on some farm
with grandparents he barely even knows! You'd be angry
too."

"But he didn't go to the farm," Eli protests. "He's at
boarding school. His parents sent him away on purpose.

That's why they won't talk to me."

I take a deep breath. "Listen, I know Randy's your friend, but I also know Randy. Who spent more time in trouble than any other kid we grew up with, including Malik? Who mouthed off to adults and even your dad? Who spent half his time in school sleeping and passing gas? Who threw a football at the Serenity Cup?" I pull the card pack out of my pocket. "Who made *these*?"

"*I* did," he says harshly. "If Randy's so terrible, then so am I. Ninety percent of what he did—I was right there with him."

I relent. "I didn't mean it that way. Randy's not terrible. But you've got to admit he wasn't the ideal Serenity kid."

"This is different."

"Don't you see?" I persist. "If this letter's the truth, it doesn't just mean the Hardaways lied. At some point, every adult in town talked to us about Randy—Mrs. Laska, your dad, Mrs. Delaney, my parents, *everybody's* parents. Did they all lie too? That would be crazy! So who's lying? Is it the people who make it possible for us to live this great life? Or is it Randy because he's sore about being sent away?"

Eli's stubborn. "Maybe that's what he means where he

says there's something screwy going on."

"Be real, Eli! Of all the things you could say about Serenity—it's a little bit small, it's a little bit conservative, it's a little bit dull. Screwy is the last thing you'd call it! I think there's something screwy going on with Randy Hardaway. It doesn't make him a bad person. But if he dreamed up a whole deck of cards just to make fun of the Purples, is it so hard to accept that he'd write one little letter to mess with you?"

"Maybe."

I think I'm finally getting through to him. But he folds up Randy's note like it's something precious, and squirrels it away in his pocket.

I'd better keep an eye on Eli. I don't like the look on his face.

7

ELI FRIEDEN

The Purple People Eater cards are a surprise hit at school.

Well, *I'm* surprised, anyway. I hang back in the corner of the classroom when Tori takes out the deck. The kids crowd around her, though, and I hear chuckles and a few out-and-out belly laughs.

"Yeah, I know that guy—the one with the giant head!"

"I saw Bigfoot a couple of days ago riding on one of the cone trucks."

"Altoiletstan—is that a real country?"

Wherever Randy is—with his grandparents or at boarding school—I can't help thinking that he must be smiling. I'm kind of proud, even though most of the funniest stuff came from him.

Even Amber can't keep the disapproving look on

her face after reading Rump L. Stiltskin's details, which are—among other things—that he was raised by a family of otters that rescued him from a freak canoeing accident, and that he can perform photosynthesis.

"Good morning!" Mrs. Laska's voice silences the laughter.

Never before have I seen index cards disappear beneath shirts and into pockets so quickly.

Luckily, Mrs. Laska doesn't seem to notice. She walks around the room, placing a crisp page facedown at each seat. "We're starting with a geometry quiz today. I have a meeting with Mr. Frieden, so I trust you all to keep your books in your desks."

As soon as she's gone, Malik has his math text open in front of him.

"She said no books," Hector stage-whispers from his seat.

"No, she didn't," Malik replies smugly. "She said 'keep your books in your desks.' My book was never in my desk. It was in my backpack."

Amber is disgusted. "Someone should make a card about you."

"Call Hardaway," he replies cheerfully. "Oh, right— he's gone."

Don't I know it.

Speaking of Randy, he's also gone from the online town records. Our town is so small that it's easy to keep a running census. The information is open access. Anyone can go on the internet and check out who lives here, who their kids are, and what their job is—except the Surety, who are kept anonymous. So Randy's out, and Serenity is down to population 184. They sure do update fast around here. I wonder if Colorado is up by one.

That night, I'm in my room on my iPad, poring over the information on the town's website. I'm not sure what I expect to find, but Randy's words pass before me like a TV news crawl:

Some of the kids are special . . .

Is it true? Or is Tori right, and it's just Randy messing with my head—a parting shot to drive me crazy while he rides off into the sunset? It wouldn't be the first time, you know. And it would be just like me to fall for it. Last night I almost said, "Randy never lied to me." But that's not true. Randy lied about the mountain lion in the crawl space under our house; he lied about seeing UFOs because we're so close to Roswell—which we aren't; he lied about seeing Mrs. Delaney hula dancing at the Purple People Eaters' luau; and, of course, he lied about the Purple

People Eaters' luau. For all I know, there was never any 1961 Alfa Romeo half buried in dust out there, and Randy just felt like a bike ride and wanted some company.

On the other hand: Randy's lies were all essentially goofs. Mostly, he lied because he was bored and wanted to stir things up a little. I can't remember him ever lying about something that really mattered. Sure, he put that giant spider in my sleeping bag. But when he found out it was poisonous, he confessed before I could get bitten. When it was important, Randy was always straight-up with me.

So what's the letter? A gag, like Tori says? I don't think Randy would joke about something like that. At the same time, his letter doesn't make a lot of sense. He said something screwy is going on, but not what. He said some of us are special, but not how. He connected it to the time I got sick, but he couldn't explain that either, or who my fellow "specials" might be.

Tori suspects she might have experienced my symptoms once. "I was at the edge of town collecting wildflowers for a painting I was working on," she told me the night we found Randy's note, "when all of a sudden I felt like I had to throw up."

"Did the Purples come?" I ask her.

"No, but it got so intense that I started home so my

parents could take me to the clinic. I've never been in so much pain!"

Brings back memories. "What did Dr. Bruder say?"

She shrugs. "I never went to him. Halfway to my house, I was totally fine again, so I figured what's the point?"

Okay, so if Tori and I are both "specials," what do we have in common?

Not much. I'm a guy; she's a girl. She has two parents; I've just got my dad. We're not the same age and grade. My father's in education, and her parents work at the plastics factory. She's a great artist while I'm happier fiddling with computers and technology.

A gust of wind blows the rain against my bedroom window, startling me back into the present moment. I'm at my desk, researching my Serenity Day project on my iPad.

Serenity isn't as dry as the desert, but real storms are rare here. Still, distant thunder has been rumbling all around us. It was only a matter of time before we got our share.

Randy on my brain, I Google McNally Academy.

There is no such place. Not in Colorado, not in any state.

Am I angry? Amused? Disappointed? Relieved?

I tip an imaginary cap to my friend. *Good one, Randy. You really had me going.*

I resolve to put the letter out of my mind and return to my Serenity Day project. I'm doing a timeline where you can see American history, New Mexico history, and Serenity history laid out side by side. This area belonged first to Spain and then to Mexico. So the birth of the USA far to the east must have seemed awfully distant to people around here.

I watch as the web page sorts itself out on my tablet.

THE BOSTON TEA PARTY

On December 16, 1773, American colonists met with representatives of the British government in Boston to discuss turning the thirteen American colonies into a separate country. Tea was served.

I write it down in my notebook, stifling a yawn. Malik always complains that Serenity is boring. Maybe that's because all American history is so boring. We're just a boring part of a boring whole, and the most interesting fact about the forming of our nation is what drink they served at the meeting.

And it took forever: 1773, and we didn't get a country until 1776? That's bureaucracy. Either that, or the Founding Fathers had to crawl on their hands and knees from Boston to Philadelphia.

There is a flash of lightning accompanied by an enormous clap of thunder that shakes the house. The lights flicker. The web page blinks out, and blinks back on again, the browser searching to reestablish a connection. It takes a few seconds as the echo of the boom dies away. The search page blinks back, reloading my Boston Tea Party options. But when I click on the top link, I'm struck by a jolt even more powerful than the lightning.

It's not the same site. The picture's the same, and the title of the article still says *The Boston Tea Party*. But the single paragraph has been replaced by dense text that fills the screen and—I scroll down—goes on to several other pages.

The Boston Tea Party was a protest against taxation without representation by the Sons of Liberty against the British government. In a dispute over three shiploads of tea, American colonists, many disguised as Mohawk warriors, boarded the ships and tossed the tea into Boston Harbor. The event was a major catalyst in bringing on the American Revolutionary War, which began with the battles of Lexington and Concord in 1775 . . .

Where did *this* web page come from? Why am I getting a different story now? And which one's true? According to this, America didn't just split off from Britain. They rebelled and fought a years-long war for independence! And they definitely didn't drink tea, because the tea was in the water.

This wasn't a friendly affair; it was a rebellion!

I'm so flabbergasted that, when the phone rings, I almost go through the ceiling. I hear my father downstairs, speaking in urgent, hushed tones. And then he's calling up the stairs to me:

"Eli, I have to run over to the school for a bit."

"In this storm?"

"That's exactly it. There have been lightning strikes around town. I have to make sure everything's all right at our building."

I stand at my window and watch him back out of the

driveway. He knows the town better than anyone. So why is he heading in the opposite direction from the school, toward the Plastics Works?

I strain to follow his taillights, but he's out of sight.

Did my father just lie to me?

I turn back to my iPad.

On December 16, 1773, American colonists met with representatives of the British government in Boston to discuss turning the thirteen American colonies into a separate country. Tea was served.

I blink. Once. Twice. It's still there. No angry colonists, no tea in the harbor, no Revolutionary War.

Okay, Mrs. Laska taught us that the internet isn't 100 percent reliable. And sometimes websites will give you slightly different versions of an event. But surely that doesn't mean a war instead of a tea party!

I fiddle with my iPad for hours that night, but I can't track down the story of the tea in Boston harbor. I search everything: *Sons of Liberty*; *taxation without representation*; *1773*. There are entries about Lexington and

Concord the *places*, but nothing about great battles happening there. When I type *American Revolutionary War*, nothing comes up.

I'm so riled that I don't even hear Dad come home. I have no idea how long he's standing behind me.

"Having technology is a privilege, Eli," he says reprovingly. "I trust you not to abuse it by staying up till all hours of the night."

Yeah, and I trust you not to tell me you're going one place and then drive off in the opposite direction!

I don't say that. I look at the clock. It's after one a.m. "Sorry," I mumble.

And that would be it. But as he walks out of the room, a spasm of anger comes over me. I'm madder at myself than I am at Dad. I mean, he's my own father, who changed my diaper when I was a baby; who loves me more than anything! Why am I so afraid to tell him what I think? What's wrong with us? What's wrong with *me*?

"Trust is a two-way street, you know," I blurt.

"I beg your pardon?"

"You said you were going to check the school. How come you turned left?"

His expression softens. "There's a lot of flooding in the

area. I had to go around the block." His gaze moves from me to my screen. The words *American Revolutionary War* are clearly visible in the search field. "You didn't happen to notice anything unusual on your tablet, did you?"

I'm astounded. "Like what?"

"The storm played havoc with a number of electrical systems around town," he explains. "I was concerned that your tablet might be damaged if you left it plugged into the charger."

"No, it's fine." I force my voice to sound calm, but inside, my mind is a blizzard of chaotic thoughts. First: *He knows.* Next: *How does he know?* And Randy's words: *Something screwy.*

If this doesn't count as screwy, I don't know what does.

And then something comes out of my mouth even I don't expect. "Dad, tell me about the Boston Tea Party."

For the first time in my memory, I see my father at a total loss for something to say. "I—I hardly think one thirty in the morning is the right time for a history lesson."

I regard my father in amazement. He looks tired, even hesitant! The steely gray eyes usually so confident betray doubt, hesitation.

Maybe it's because I've got the Boston Tea Party on the brain, but I experience this amazing thrill of, well, *independence.* It's a genuine rush, and it leads me to make a terrible mistake.

I pull Randy's letter out of my pocket, unfold it, and slam it into his hand.

8
MALIK BRUDER

I don't have many good things to say about Happy Valley, New Mexico, but here's one: we don't get a lot of thunderstorms.

Which does me no good tonight, because this is a big one. The flashes light up the town like it's high noon, and the crashes are beyond just loud. You feel them inside your skull.

The worst part is I'm sitting on my bed, rocking back and forth, praying for it to be over, and I know that Hector, who's afraid of moths, loves electrical storms! Well, he must be thrilled tonight, because this one is blowing the lid off New Mexico!

It finally dies out after midnight. But before I can calm down and go to sleep, we get a telephone call. Dad's the only doctor in town, so this must be a medical emergency.

I stick my head into the hall. I can almost feel the wind from my dad hustling into his clothes behind the master bedroom door. And my parents' "whispered" conversation sounds more like shouting. I'm dying to know what's going on. Something's up; something big.

The door flies open, and I catch my father's parting words to Mom. ". . . by the time we get through with him, it'll be the truth." He wheels around, and that's when he sees me standing there. "Go back to bed, Malik."

"Who's sick?"

"I suppose you'll hear about it tomorrow anyway. It's Eli Frieden."

"Is it bad?" I ask

"It's not good. He's had a relapse of his recent illness."

I can tell it's not good. Dad's leaving the house without one of his dumb bow ties, which happens about once per millennium. It usually takes an outbreak of plague for that.

"Is it—serious?"

"He's not going to die, if that's what you mean," my father replies. "I have to go."

My mother wraps her arms around me as the door

closes downstairs. "Don't worry, honey. I'm sure your friend will be fine."

I bristle. "What planet are you living on, Mom? I'm not his nursemaid; I'm not even his friend. I hate everybody equally."

She's used to me. "You're all close friends, all thirty of you."

"Twenty-nine, but who's counting?" I mumble.

"I forgot about Randy." She hugs me tighter. "That must have been upsetting to you—"

"I already told you it wasn't."

"—and now this on top of that."

Even if we lived in a city, with millions of mothers in it, mine would still be the most annoying. I just want to twist out of her suffocating embrace. But I don't, because she has a point.

I *shouldn't* care about Eli, but I do. What choice do I have? In Happy Valley, we're all basically stuck with each other.

The next day at school, Stanley Cole and Melanie Brandt are trading Purple People Eater cards—Rump L. Stiltskin for Sunshine plus Dodecahedron Face.

I'm totally blown away. "Why?"

"Stiltskin's worth two," Stanley explains. "He performs photosynthesis."

"So does your lawn," I point out.

"I like Dodecahedron Face," says Melanie. "I see him near my house sometimes. He's cute."

"Cute?" Tori challenges. "His head is shaped like a dodecahedron!"

"What's a dodecahedron?" I ask irritably. "Wait, scratch that. I don't care. Listen, Frieden's not coming to school today. He had a relapse of pukey-pukey last night."

"Is it serious?" Tori probes.

I shrug dramatically. Dad finally rolled in this morning while I was getting ready for school. If there was bad news, he would have told me then. "Well, the Purples didn't have to drag him home this time. He was home already."

Amber shoots me a disapproving look. "You don't have to be so mean about it."

"Lighten up," I shoot back. "He's not dead. He probably just wishes he was."

Hector's uncertain. "Your dad never figured out what was wrong with Eli the first time around."

I glare at him. "Are you saying my father's a lousy doctor?"

He backs off. "No, Malik! Not at all! It's just—if we

don't know what it is, how do we know it isn't contagious?"

"That's right, Hector, think about yourself," Amber scolds. "Remember, community is sharing."

"That's what I'm worried about!" Hector defends himself. "I don't want him to share it with me! Malik, what does your dad say it is?"

"None of your business," I grumble. "He doesn't talk about patients." Dad's exact words were *"by the time we get through with him, it'll be the truth."* That sounds more like a threat than a diagnosis. But doctors don't go around threatening patients. Mostly it makes no sense at all.

"Randy," Tori whispers resentfully.

We stare at her. "What are you talking about?" Amber asks. "Randy left two weeks ago. What could he have to do with Eli getting sick now?"

She hesitates, like she's struggling over whether or not to tell us. Once she starts singing, though, it's a real opera. "He left a letter for Eli that really freaked him out. He says he isn't with his grandparents. He's been shipped off to some boarding school. He thinks there's some kind of plot going on in Serenity. Or maybe it's not a plot—it's just weird. His exact words were 'something screwy.'" The longer she goes on, the more upset she gets. "And it's all because some of us are supposed to be special!"

"Special *how?*" asks Amber in bewilderment.

"It's a goof!" I snort, laughing it off. "Hardaway was always a wing nut, and this was his way of leaving us with something to remember him by. What a doofus."

"But Eli refuses to believe that," Tori tells us. "He thinks there's something going on in Serenity, and we all could be in danger. And now look what's happened to him!"

"You don't get sick from being upset," Hector insists. "Something has to be really wrong with you."

We have Squatting and Mumbling first that day, which is what I call Meditation. I make fun of it, but it's actually my favorite subject in school. Who can argue with a class where you do nothing, there are no assignments, and it's impossible to prove you didn't finish your homework? But as I sit cross-legged on my carpet square that day, I'm meditating for real, or at least thinking pretty hard. Just because Hardaway's a joker doesn't necessarily mean he's joking now. I don't know any special people, and I couldn't care less if he's at a boarding school or a farm or on the surface of Pluto. But those words—*something screwy*—ring a bell with me.

Ever since the day Hector bled all over that shipment of traffic cones, I've been keeping an eye on those trucks.

I swear I saw dark crusty stains on one of them yesterday! Am I imagining things? Or is that the same load of cones?

What could the point of driving a shipment of cones around town for all these weeks possibly be?

Screwy.

After Meditation, Mrs. Laska announces, "Let's each of us think of a message we'd like to put on Eli's get-well card."

I write *Feel better, man,* but what I really want to say is *Be careful, Eli.* I don't like what my father said. And maybe Randy's not such a wing nut after all.

What if I've spent so much of my life complaining about how small and boring and one-horse Serenity is that I've missed the forest for the trees?

This place is messed up, and nobody knows it better than me.

9

ELI FRIEDEN

It's like I'm swimming, up, up, trying to reach the surface, trying to breathe. Bubbles race all around me. Why can't I speed up? Then I see the heavy weights attached to my ankles. It's impossible to make any progress, and yet I keep at it, flailing my arms and kicking with all my might.

The urge to breathe is more than a desire; it's a mania, the kind of primal urge that takes over mind and body and blocks out all other thought. My vision darkens around the edges. The oxygen deprivation is getting to me now. I'm not going to make it. But I can't stop moving because, the instant I do, the weights will drag me down to the bottom. How far below? I can't know. All that matters is going up.

Just as my lungs are about to explode, I break the

surface in a cascade of spray, gasping in great gulps of air. When at last my lungs are satisfied, I scan my surroundings, praying for rescue.

A huge shape looms above me. It's a British frigate, riding at anchor in the harbor. I crane my neck for a better look. There are men on board, in Mohawk warrior garb. The first chest of tea hits the water barely a few feet from me.

I find my voice at last. "Help!"

The tea keeps raining all around me.

"Hey, over here!"

A figure on board peers down at me. Beneath the disguise, I recognize Randy's familiar face. He calls something to me. What's he saying?

"There's something screwy going on in that town!"

"What is it?" I beg.

He opens his mouth to speak again, but at that moment, my strength deserts me, and I'm sinking again. My last thought before the darkness claims me again is a single word:

Remember . . .

My class sends me a potted geranium as a get-well gift.

It's dying.

Dad frowns. "I don't understand why it isn't doing better. All the other plants around the house are thriving."

Right, Dad. That's what we need to be talking about. Horticulture.

"Maybe it just needs more sunlight," I suggest, propping myself higher on my pillow.

He looks dubious but pushes the pot a little closer to my window. "Time for your medicine, Eli." He puts three capsules into my hand and sets a glass of water on the nightstand.

I slug back the pills like a pro. I've had enough practice this past week, three times a day, Dr. Bruder's orders.

My father carefully watches me drink down all the water. "I'm proud of you, Eli. You've been an excellent patient." He smiles warmly, squeezes my shoulder, and heads downstairs to catch up on some emails. He's been working from home ever since I've been put on bed rest.

He's right, actually. I'm an awesome patient. As soon as I hear him on the stairs, I spit out the three capsules I stored in my cheek and bury them in the soil of the geranium. That's what the thing's dying of—a drug overdose. I'm not even sure what's in those pills except that they make me groggy and confused. A couple of days in, I lie in bed, struggling to remember something. It's just at the edge of my consciousness, so close I should be able to reach out and grab it.

Then I realize what it is.

Randy's letter.

They're trying to make me forget about it.

No, not some faceless "they." *He.* Felix Frieden. My one and only parent.

Why, Dad? Why?

I can't describe how awful it is. I'm physically sick— it's almost as bad as that time on my bike.

One minute you think you've got your life figured out. The next it shatters like a glass bowl hitting a stone patio.

My own father is the enemy.

Anyway, that's when I stopped taking the pills. Trust me, there is no feeling quite so lonely as learning you have no one who will always be on your side. It's the ultimate loneliness because you are exactly that: alone. My sole ally, my only friend, is my mind. I have to keep it clear, because all I have now is my understanding of what's happening to me.

I can't decide what's scarier: that Dad and Dr. Bruder want me to forget Randy's note, or that they're actually capable of it.

Speaking of Dr. Bruder, he comes every day to check on my progress. He's his usual goofy self, performing card tricks while he examines me. Every kid in Serenity is familiar with the experience of having to answer the question "Is this your card" while there's a tongue depressor shoved far enough down your throat to tickle your belly button. Then there are the jokes: "How about we take out your tonsils? It's a two-for-one special today. No extra charge." You are required to laugh or he keeps them coming. He prefers a big guffaw, but today he'll have to settle for a chuckle. He should understand better than anyone how groggy I must be. He's the one prescribing the pills I'm not taking.

But today the shtick falls flatter than usual, because nothing can cover how closely he's watching me. Another difference: my father is always in on these examinations, and if Dr. Bruder's gaze is intense, Dad's is a laser beam.

They ask me how I'm feeling about fifty times, and I tell them what I think they want to hear: yes, I feel better, kind of sleepy. But no, there's no pain or nausea.

I'll always remember those afternoons as the time that I leave Serenity for good. Not physically, of course. But that's when the whole idea of the town—the honesty, harmony, and contentment—ceases to have any meaning for me. I'm lying to them, and I don't even feel bad about it, because I know they're lying to me. It may look like harmony in my room, but that's all phony. And for sure, I'm not feeling very content about it.

"Do you recall the moment you got sick?" Dr. Bruder probes.

"Not really," I reply. That's the only thing I say that's true. I don't remember getting sick, because I never *was* sick. My father probably put something in the hot chocolate we had that night to help us both sleep after our argument. I don't mention the argument. I think that's one of the things I'm supposed to forget. "I know it was the night of the big storm, but I don't remember much after that."

"How did the pills make you feel?"

"Groggy," I reply. "But I started feeling better right away. You know, happier. Less stressed." I don't mention that it made me feel terrific when I dug them out of the plant an hour ago and flushed them down the toilet.

It hurts to lie, but not half as much as the reason *why* I'm lying. That my father has turned on me, and that everything I believed to be true—all the Serenity stuff— is not what it seems.

The doctor smiles. "Well, I have good news for you.

Eli. You're on the mend. It was probably just a relapse of your previous condition, brought on by the change in atmospheric pressure from the storm."

"Great." I have to give him credit. He can make total hooey sound like real doctoring.

"One more thing." My father steps forward and holds out a piece of paper. "Do you recognize this?"

I know exactly what it is. It's a line drawing of an old-time British ship, and it comes straight from the website on the Boston Tea Party—the one about the rebellion and the colonists throwing tea into the water, and the American Revolutionary War.

"It's a boat," I say in the most clueless voice I can manage. "An old-fashioned ship. Should I recognize it?"

My father leans over and hugs me. "Welcome back, Eli," he says in an emotional tone.

My first visitor is Mrs. Delaney. She takes me for a stroll in the backyard. Actually, it's awesome. I haven't set foot out the door in days.

"We've been missing you at the pool," she says kindly. "Especially Malik."

I smile. "Oh yeah. He's really the tenderhearted type."

"Well, you're the only one with the talent to stand

up to him. Now he doesn't know who to bean first." She turns serious. "It's good to see you back on your feet. We were all worried. It must have been scary."

"Not really."

"Still, you were so sick the last time. And to have it all come back . . ."

I'm listening to her with one ear. Mostly, though. I'm listening to the churning inside my brain:

Mrs. Delaney is an outsider. Until six months ago, she was a regular person in a regular town . . .

I can't be sure if it's safe to tell her the things I have to share with someone. But if not her, then who? Definitely not any other adult. It's her or nobody.

"Can I talk to you?" I say suddenly.

She's startled. "Of course. We *are* talking."

"I mean can I tell you something that you can't repeat to anyone else—not my dad, not even your husband in the Purp—the Surety?"

She hesitates. "I don't know, Eli. I'm new here. But the way I read it, people don't keep secrets in Serenity."

Of course they do! For starters, you have no idea that your husband's card has already been traded four times, maybe more! This place is practically the Secrets capital of the world!

Aloud, I just say, "Some of them do."

She mulls this over. "I guess that's the first secret—that there are secrets."

I keep my mouth shut. I've probably blabbed too much already. I like Mrs. Delaney, but she's married to a Purple People Eater. If I say something and it gets back to Dad, I'll be on bed rest again. And this time there might not be a potted geranium to take the pills for me.

"Well, don't keep me in suspense," she prompts with one of her friendly grins. "You can't tell me that, and then be a clam."

I have to say it. Otherwise I'll chicken out. "Promise me I can trust you."

She's quiet for a moment, and then, "It seems to me that you kids could use someone to talk to. If you choose me to be that someone, I'm flattered. But I can't guarantee anything if you're putting yourself in danger."

I just blurt it out. "I wasn't sick. Not this time, anyway."

She's taken aback. "But why—?"

"Dr. Bruder's giving me pills. I'm only pretending to take them."

"Eli, are you sure that's smart?" she asks with concern. "Dr. Bruder wouldn't give you pills unless you need them."

"Look at me. I'm fine!" I do a few jumping jacks.

"Enough—I get it!" She regards me earnestly. "I want to help you, but I'm not sure I understand what all this is about."

"I'm starting to learn things about this town," I say slowly, "and I think they're trying to make me forget."

She looks at me skeptically. "What is it that you've learned?"

My heart sinks. The disappointment almost knocks me over. "Don't *you* know?"

Her expressive face radiates deep sympathy, and she reaches over and gives me a friendly hug. "You're having a tough time, Eli, and that's partly because you're growing up without a mom. If there's ever anything you need to talk about, you can always depend on me."

She's the only adult in town I can trust. And she thinks I'm nuts.

Maybe she's right.

10

TORI PRITEL

Eli hasn't been to school for two weeks, and no one's been allowed to visit him. I go with Amber and her mom to deliver the get-well plant, but we aren't invited inside. When I phone over there, Mr. Frieden tells me his son is asleep. No one sleeps that much, not even if they get bitten by an African tsetse fly.

"Is it serious?" I ask.

"It's quite serious, I'm afraid, Victoria," Mr. Frieden replies gravely. "But don't worry. He's receiving excellent care."

Don't worry? (I'm obviously worrying!)

"What is it?" I ask in a small voice.

"A relapse of the illness he suffered a few weeks ago."

"Well, can I come and see him? I promise I won't wake him up."

"Sadly, no visitors. But I'll tell him you called." He hangs up.

Everybody's worried about Eli, but it's obvious that I'm the most worried, and Malik won't let me hear the end of it.

"You li-i-ike him," he singsongs at me.

"Of course I like him! We all like him! We've known each other since we were babies!"

"Sure, Tori. And you lo-o-o-oved him as a baby too," Malik snickers.

U like him is on the note I find in my jacket pocket and on the tiny crumpled paper that bounces off the back of my head in Meditation. *I Love Eli* is the new subject line in all my composition books.

Amber puts a stop to the harassment by stomping on Malik's foot.

"Are you crazy, Laska?" he yells, hopping up and down.

Once the heat of the moment has passed, Amber is shamefaced. "I can't believe I resorted to violence. Nobody does that. Not even Malik."

"You were awesome," I tell her. "Besides, it was only his toe."

"And that makes a difference?" she laments. "It's not how much harm you cause. It's that you do it at all."

That comes straight out of our Contentment book. Which explains why this incident is kind of a big deal. While Malik puts his toe on ice, watching it swell up black-and-blue, Mrs. Laska hauls her daughter to the principal's office. Long story short, Amber's Contentment midterm is reduced a full grade, from A-plus to B-plus.

"A *B*!" she laments. "I've never had a B in my whole life!"

"It worked, though," I remind her. "Malik's totally left me alone ever since."

"You're welcome," she says. "Now *you* can leave *me* alone while I work on getting my average back up. And this isn't helping with my goal weight either. You know I snack when I'm stressed."

She doesn't come with me when I walk by Eli's house hoping to catch a glimpse of him through a window.

But I don't see him. What I *do* see is a Purple People Eater hunched in a parked car across the street from the Frieden home. (Tomfoolerus Dingbat. Hobbies: squeezing blackheads and world domination.)

It's funny. You almost never see Purples around town. Their focus is on the Plastics Works. Why are they watching

Eli's house? If he's sick, he needs doctors, not sentries.

I can't help but think back to the note we found in Randy's pool filter, the one I was so sure was a joke. Well, I'm not laughing anymore. I don't know if Randy's on a farm or at a school, or if there are "special" people in Serenity, or even if I might be one of them.

But there is one part of Randy's letter that I agree with 100 percent. There really does seem to be something screwy going on in this town! I don't even care that much about what it is. I just want Eli back, safe and sound.

And then one day, there he is.

". . . one nation under God, indivisible, with unity and gladness for all."

We're just finishing the Pledge of Allegiance when Eli walks into the classroom. I've practically forgotten what he looks like. But he looks good. Better yet, he looks fine—completely healthy. We all jump up to welcome him. I want to throw my arms around him, but one glance at Malik tells me to hang back. (I don't think Amber could handle another blow to her Contentment grade.)

"All right, settle down," says Mrs. Laska, smiling. "Take your seats, everybody. You too, Eli. Today, you're the guest of honor."

"Thanks for the plant," he says sheepishly. "It died."

"We're just happy to have you back. Now, turn to page 214 . . ."

I don't get a chance to talk to Eli until lunch, and then I can't find him. In a school of twenty-nine, this is ridiculous. I wander all over the schoolyard and finally locate him in the trees. He's in the middle of an animated conversation with Malik—not my favorite person these days.

Their faces are flushed, their arms waving. But as soon as I get there, they clam up. It's pretty obvious that my arrival has interrupted something important.

"Scram," Malik tells me. Always the diplomat.

I ignore him and focus on Eli. "Tell me what happened to you."

"You saw Randy's letter," he says stiffly. "You didn't believe it."

I stare at him. "What does the letter have to do with being sick?"

"I *wasn't* sick. I showed the note to my father and he spent the next two weeks feeding me full of pills to make me forget it ever existed."

"Where would he get pills like that?"

He points at Malik. "From *his* dad! They were in on it together!"

Astounded, I turn to Malik. "And you're fighting with him for accusing your father?"

"I'm not fighting with him!" Malik defends himself. "This is how I talk! I was trying to tell him something when you barged in, so take a hike."

"Why can't I hear it too?" I demand.

"Because if Randy's letter made you go all clammy, you're not going to be too thrilled with what I have to say."

"I—" I hesitate. "Maybe I'm not so sure about that anymore."

"I just spent two weeks flat on my back, spitting pills into a potted plant," Eli says bitterly. "And I'll be right back there if my dad finds out about this conversation."

I'm appalled. "I would never tell on you!"

"Maybe *you* wouldn't," Malik counters, "but what if you confide in your soul sister, Amber? She's the biggest fangirl Happy Valley ever had!"

"That's not fair—" As soon as the words are out of my mouth, though, I realize he's right. Poor Amber is losing her mind over a B-plus. Her mother has her on double Meditation because she stomped on Malik's toe. We've all bought into what our parents and teachers have told us, but Amber's the most devoted. If she thinks we're conspiring against the Serenity way of life, she'll blow the whistle on us for sure.

"I won't tell her. I swear." Part of me can't believe I'm promising to keep something from my best friend.

Malik looks to Eli, who nods his approval.

"I don't think the plastics factory makes very many traffic cones," Malik says evenly.

Of all the things I expect, this has to be dead last. "How can you say that? There are truckloads of them being hauled out of town every day!"

Malik shakes his head. "I thought so too. But if you look close, they've only got three trucks—four, tops. It seems like more because they never go anywhere. They just drive around Happy Valley, lugging the same cones. They've been at it for weeks. Maybe for years."

"How could you know that?"

He explains about the skateboarding accident and how the stains from Hector's nosebleed are still on the shipment. "I'm not as positive about the other trucks, but I'm starting to recognize them—you know, a dent here, a scratch there. No way have they got more than three or four. And the cones aren't freshly made product—not all covered in dust like that."

My head is spinning. "But my *parents* work at that

plant! And not just mine—it supports the whole town!"

"I'm starting to suspect that a lot of the information we get might be wrong," Eli puts in. "I had a pretty weird experience on the internet during that storm. I got two completely different web pages on the same topic. I mean *really* different."

I must seem stunned, because Malik shoots me a look. "Heard enough yet?"

"Something's not right, something very basic to this town and our lives," Eli says earnestly. "And whatever it is, all our parents seem to be mixed up in it."

My head is pounding and my pulse is racing. What happened to Eli is scary, but that can be blamed on two people—Mr. Frieden and Dr. Bruder. But the Plastics Works is *everybody*—every adult in town—including Steve and Elizabeth Pritel!

Mom and Dad, who spoil me, who spent a fortune finishing the attic so I could have an art studio! Dad, who calls me Torific, and tells me I'm the princess of his heart! They go to that factory every day and come home and talk about the traffic cone business!

Is it all a lie? "There must be some explanation—"

Malik reads my mind. "Don't even think about asking your parents! They're up to their necks in this, just like everybody else. That's rule number one—no parents!"

Eli regards me kindly. "You can still back out, you know, Tori. We trust you to keep this secret."

Secrets. Lies. Those used to be dirty words, alien customs of an outside world we don't have to worry about here. How could so much have changed so quickly? Oh, how I wish I could roll back the last month and erase all this craziness.

But it's too late for that.

I have one final question for them. "What do you mean 'back out'? Back out of what?"

Eli mulls this over a moment. "Well, we can't ask anybody, because we can't trust anybody. If we want to get to the bottom of this, we're going to have to do it on our own."

"Now you're talking," Malik approves. "Where do we start?"

They stare at each other, and it's obvious they've thought not an inch beyond deciding to take action.

To my surprise, the voice that breaks the silence is my own. "We start with the one thing we know for sure—the Plastics Works. If they're not making traffic cones, what *are* they doing in there?"

11

ELI FRIEDEN

It takes a few days for things to get back to normal around our house. Eventually, though, life resumes its regular boring rhythm. Boring is good. My father likes order and sameness, which makes it hard for him to peek into my room and check on me at all hours of the night. Soon I'm the one checking on him. He sleeps like a baby, and snores like a buzz saw.

That's when I give the go-ahead to put our plan into action.

Every time I think about what I'm doing, I feel like my head's going to explode. That's when I remind myself of what my dad and Dr. Bruder did to me. It's always good for a surge of courage.

Serenity isn't the liveliest place in the middle of the

day. At night you could safely roll a giant boulder up Amity Avenue without putting anybody in danger. And at two o'clock in the morning, it's dark and silent as a tomb.

I ease myself out through the back door, convinced that I'm going to be the only one crazy enough to report for this expedition. The kids of Serenity follow the rules 100 percent. The town charter has no provision for sneaking around.

The meeting place is under the big maple tree at the corner of Amity and Fellowship. I'm equal parts amazed and relieved to find Tori there waiting for me. She seems terrified.

"I thought for sure it would be just me," she says, a slight tremor in her voice.

"Me too. Where's Malik?" I'm wondering if something went wrong—a medical issue somewhere in town that would have Dr. Bruder awake and about. We have no backup plan. Do we go home or continue on as a twosome? The thought of weaseling out of this is more attractive than I'd like to admit.

But no such luck. I make out a hulking dark figure approaching along Amity.

"Sorry I'm late," Malik greets us. He may be big and tough, but he looks twice as scared as we are.

The three of us start down the Fellowship hill toward the chimneys of the Plastics Works. It's a moonless night, so dark that when you step away from somebody, the face disappears almost immediately. We might as well be in deep space.

The factory is absolutely still—a shadow that could just as easily be a small mountain as a building. There are only a handful of lights, none of them much brighter than a bug zapper. Considering this is supposed to be a major manufacturing corporation, it sure looks like nobody's home.

We don't see the perimeter fence until we're almost upon it. It's eight feet high, and seems even higher in the darkness. We begin to circle the property, looking for a way in. At last, we arrive at the electronic gate. Three traffic cone trucks are parked on the roadway just inside.

"There could be others," Tori suggests. "You know, out of town making deliveries."

"You guys want to see Hector's blood?" Malik offers.

"We'll take your word for it," I decide.

As far as I know, no kid has ever been inside the Plastics Works. The plant is off-limits except to employees, and there are no open houses or take-your-children-to-work days. That's what makes the next step so difficult. Once past that gate, there's no pleading innocence or playing dumb. Everybody knows it's forbidden territory. Worse, the plant is Purple People Eater country. We may make fun of their big teeth and photosynthesis, but nobody wants to tangle with them.

The gate is a little shorter than the fence—perhaps seven feet. Climbing over it feels like passing a point of no return. When we jump to the ground, the impact of our shoes on the gravel resounds like fireworks, and we scramble to the dirt path as quickly as we can.

Another crunch—a footstep? Is somebody there? A hand squeezes my wrist. It's Tori, her face ghostly white.

I count silently—ten seconds, then twenty.

"False alarm," I whisper.

We scamper toward the building itself, taking a quick inventory of all doors and windows. Our plan is simple: Find a window, look inside. Are they making traffic cones? What else are they doing? If we can't see anything in the first window, we move on to the next, and so on.

But the closer we get, the more it becomes apparent that the windows are a lot farther up than they appear from the road. There's no way we could boost one of us high enough to get a look in there, not even standing on each other's shoulders. And anyway, we're not circus performers.

There's a loading bay, but the heavy folding door is padlocked shut.

"What about this?" suggests Malik. He reaches for the handle of the only other way in on this side of the building, a metal door marked *Keep Out*.

"Freeze!" Tori rasps.

"I doubt it's open," I put in.

Tori points to the top corner of the doorframe. Two tiny strands of color run from the brick into the metal. "It's wired for an alarm. There might even be a sensor on the knob itself."

We stare at her. Where did *that* come from? I mean, I'm grateful that she saved us from a potential mistake, but how did she *see* it? People don't even lock their doors in Serenity. What gave Tori the eagle eyes to spot an inch and a half of alarm wire?

"We can't touch anything," I decide.

"Great," grumbles Malik. "So we risked a heap of trouble to come here and do what? Nothing."

None of us has an answer for that. We're standing there like idiots, when the noise reaches us—a soft electric motor. The thought of Purple People Eaters jolts us into action. There's only one place to go—a low stand of shrubbery against the wall of the factory. We practically trample each other, scrambling into shelter just as a golf cart makes the turn around the corner of the factory and comes into view.

Flashlight beams crisscross the ground in a rhythmic pattern. My eyes follow the cones of light to their source on the cart—the indigo uniforms of the Surety.

Nobody breathes. Trembling, we crouch amid the scratchy branches as the beams sweep over us. The tension is like a fog surrounding us. I recognize one of the Purples' faces—Screaming Mimi. And the other—I squint to see past the brightness of the bulb—Alexander the Grape.

What difference does it make which ones they are? If they catch us, it's the end of the world!

In my mind, we're impossible to overlook—three clumsy bodies trying to disappear behind a few brambles.

And then the flashlights move on past. The patrol continues to parallel the wall and disappears around the far end of the complex.

It's only when the sound of the cart's motor has completely faded that we muster the courage to emerge from the bush, one figure at a time—one . . . two . . . three . . . four . . .

Four?!

Frantic, I identify Tori and Malik. Someone else is here too! I can see him in silhouette.

Were we so worried about the Purples in the cart that we didn't notice the one hiding three feet away from us?

Tori and I stand frozen, but Malik doesn't freeze so easily. Like a panther, he lunges at the stranger, hauling him up by the scruff of the neck.

"Ow, Malik, that hurts!"

Hector.

Malik is furious. "Where do you get off following us here?"

Hector stands up to him. "I didn't follow *them*; I followed *you*! Why are you leaving me out?"

"You think this is some kind of game?" Malik demands.

Hector spreads his arms wide. "Whatever it is, I can help you guys!"

"No!" Malik rasps. "You'll treat this like a club you want to join. And then you'll get scared—"

"I won't! I swear! I'm a part of this!"

Malik is beside himself. "If you don't know what it is,

how do you know you're a part of it?"

I have a thought. "Randy's note said some of us are special. It could be Hector as much as any of us."

"Yeah, I'm special," Hector says, pleased. "Special how?"

"We'll explain later," Tori assures him. "Let's get out of here."

From my jacket pocket I pull out my iPad, and snap pictures of the loading bay, the *Keep Out* door, and the high windows. "Maybe we'll notice something that we missed," I explain.

I'm about to slide the tablet back into my jacket when I see something that makes me frown. Along the bottom of my screen, right beside the battery indicator, I spot the icon for Wi-Fi. Why would I have Wi-Fi? I'm too far from home where our router is, and there are no other houses here, so I can't be piggybacking on someone else's network. This Wi-Fi has to be coming from the factory!

I open the browser, and a pop-up appears, asking for a security code.

I'm a little surprised, since we don't use passwords a lot in Serenity. We know what they *are*—our parents order things from online stores from time to time. But I've never seen the internet itself protected by a PIN.

The others gather around, offering suggestions. "Try *Serenity*," Malik supplies. "Around here, every toilet is stuffed up with that name."

I type it in. *ACCESS DENIED.*

"How about *plastic*?" Hector puts in. "Or *plastics works?*"

ACCESS DENIED.

"Maybe *Honesty*?" Tori offers. "*Harmony? Contentment?*"

We test them all—every word or phrase we've ever heard associated with our town—*Serenity Cup, Pax, traffic cones, factory*, and the last names of every town official. No luck.

Then I notice something. The sign-in page isn't all that different from the screen that's on display when I hack into my Xbox. If Randy and I can exploit glitches in our video games . . .

A few taps later, I'm probing into the actual HTML coding of the web page. Most of it's gibberish—long strings of letters, numbers, and symbols. But in the middle of all that programming stew is a single word I recognize: *Hammerstrom.*

"Hammerstrom?" Malik repeats. "What's that?"

"One of the Purples," I reply. "But if he's the guy who

set up the portal, maybe he used his own name as a PIN."

I backtrack out of the coding until I see the password page again. My hands are trembling as I type the letters into the field: *HAMMERSTROM*.

We hear a beep, and there's the Google home page. We're in!

The whirr of the golf cart is audible again. It's the patrol coming around to make another pass. The others duck back into the bush, but I'm frozen to the spot, tapping the virtual keyboard.

"What are you doing, man?" Malik hisses. "Get down! We've got company!"

I'm still typing as if my fingers are moving on their own: *BOSTON TEA PARTY*.

Malik reaches out and drags me backward into the bushes just as the golf cart rounds the corner. Tori smacks the tablet against my chest, dousing the glow of the screen. We suspend breathing. Bushes don't breathe.

The crisscrossing flashlight beams swing over us. The Purple People Eaters move on again.

"You idiot!" Malik rages in an undertone. "What was so important to see on there? Are you checking your fantasy football team?"

I pull the iPad out and show it to them.

THE BOSTON TEA PARTY

The Boston Tea Party was a protest against taxation without representation by the Sons of Liberty against the British government . . .

"This website came up for me during the storm!" I explain to them. "Compare this with what they taught us—that the colonists and the British drank tea and decided to form a new country."

"I don't care!" Malik is still angry. "You almost got us caught!"

Light dawns on Hector first. "They're tampering with our internet!"

"Who's 'they'?" asks Tori. "The Purple People Eaters?"

"They're just the enforcers," I reply.

"Mrs. Laska!" Hector breathes. He turns to me. "And your dad!"

"It's worse than that," I tell him. "The Purples, everybody who works at the school, or the factory—"

"Our parents!" moans Tori.

"It's the whole lot of them," Malik adds angrily. "Every adult in Happy Valley."

"Right," I agree. "And if they control our internet, and they control our school, and they control our town, then we can't trust anything we think we know about our lives!"

There's dead silence as this sinks in.

Hector has a question. "But if our internet is phony, how come it isn't phony here?"

I'm guessing at the answer, but it makes perfect sense. "Because this is the *factory's* internet, leaking out through the walls. They want the real thing in there. Whatever's going on in Serenity, I'll bet it's being controlled from inside this building."

On a whim, I tap two more words into the search field: *McNALLY ACADEMY.*

McNally Academy is a private coeducational boarding school located outside the town of Pueblo, Colorado. Founded in 1954 . . .

"Randy," Tori whispers. "He was telling the truth."

There's no way my absent friend could hear me, yet somehow it feels important that I say it aloud. "I never should have doubted you, man."

Malik slaps the bricks of the Plastics Works. "We have

to find a way to get in there."

It's funny—we've snuck out, trespassed on factory property, hunkered down like criminals, hidden from the Surety. Yet Malik's words scare me more than anything else that's happened tonight.

It doesn't make sense. The risky part is almost over. Why am I suddenly unable to control my runaway breathing?

Maybe it's this: nothing is over.

This is just the beginning.

12

TORI PRITEL

The instant I step inside the house, the projectile strikes me dead center in the forehead, landing on the tiles at my feet.

"Steve—" My mother's voice is exasperated.

"Shhh!" Dad hisses urgently. "This is a delicate operation. It requires the utmost concentration . . ." Another shot is coming toward me. I open my mouth to catch it, but it bounces off my chin and hits the floor beside the first miss.

When I reach down to pick them up, my father stops me with a wagging finger. "Uh-uh-uh. There's an art to this. An artist like you should understand that." He takes another piece of caramel popcorn from the bowl and tosses it in my direction.

It's a good throw, but it bounces off my teeth as I try to snap it out of the air.

"You'll attract every bug in New Mexico," Mom warns, but she's smiling.

Dad's next attempt is wide to my left, but I'm able to catch it with my mouth. We celebrate (". . . another Torific reception . . . !") and Mom doesn't even say anything when I scarf down the first three missed attempts. (Our house is so clean you really *can* eat off the floor.)

"Where were you, honey?" she asks.

"Oh, just at the park."

"Who with?" Dad probes.

"Eli and Malik," I reply carefully. "Hector was there too."

"Amber stopped by, looking for you," Mom informs me. "I'd assumed you were with her."

I try to sound casual. "No, not this time."

This is the hardest part—not that I'm plotting to break every rule of the only place I've ever known, but that I don't dare tell my closest friend.

Amber suspects something's up, and it really hurts not to be able to confide in her. But I don't dare, and not just because I promised the guys. What we learned at the factory the other night is something she could never accept.

So I can't tell her—not until I have real proof. The problem is: proof of *what*? We know that things are being kept from us, and our internet's different, and the factory isn't exactly what it's supposed to be. But that's not the same as understanding *why*. Yes, we're being deceived, but what's the purpose of the deception? What is the "something screwy" Randy warned us about?

"What about our project?" Amber demands. "How are we ever going to get it finished by Serenity Day?"

"Don't worry," I assure her. "Once I get the faces right, the rest of the mural should be a breeze."

She obviously notices that I'm not around as much, but I don't think she suspects who I'm with instead. And the fact that the four of us are planning a break-in—well, that's something she can't ever know.

It goes without saying that we're not experts. (In Serenity, the only thing we learn about breaking and entering is that it's someone else's problem, somewhere far, far away.) I draw a map of the entire town, detailing every single building, house, and flagpole. We walk, bike, scooter, skateboard, Rollerblade, and even pogo stick every inch of the place in search of a fresh view of the Plastics Works that might reveal a way in that we haven't thought of yet.

Here's what we've come up with so far:

1) *Find a thirty-foot ladder and try for a window.* Flaws: window may be wired to an alarm; impossible to estimate drop to factory floor; no place to hide ladder from Surety patrol. Plus, this is a small town with no tall buildings. If anyone has use for a ladder that big, it would be the Plastics Works themselves. And we obviously can't ask them if we can borrow it.

2) *Splice extensions into the existing alarm wires in order to bypass the door.* Flaws: not sure how to cut the wire to splice it without setting off the alarm in the first place. And even if that's possible, we'd still need to pick the door lock quickly enough to avoid the patrol (not a skill they teach at our school).

3) *One of us stows away on the golf cart and is driven inside by the Purple People Eaters themselves.* Flaws: golf carts aren't limousines; there's no place to hide and very little clearance underneath. Also, we have no evidence that the golf cart ever enters the building.

"In other words, we've got nothing," Eli concludes sadly.

"Not necessarily," I muse. "What about the roof?"

"The *roof*?" Malik repeats incredulously. "If we can't reach the windows, how can we get up to the roof?"

"The windows are harder because they're exposed," I explain reasonably. "The patrol can spot us from the golf cart. But once we're up on the roof, we're out of sight. And we've got all the time in the world to find a way in."

"We can't even *see* the roof," Hector points out. "How are we going to know if there's access to the building?"

"No problem," Malik says sarcastically. "I'll just ask the Purples if we can borrow their helicopter."

"He's got a point," Eli admits. "There's not a place in town high enough for a view of the factory roof. Not even the flagpole."

"What about the online archives?" I wonder. Steve showed me how to access them on my computer. There are all kinds of images of the town and the surrounding area, some of them really cool. "Maybe there's an aerial photograph."

"We've already checked," says Malik. "They've got pictures and schematics and blueprints of every building in Happy Valley *except* the Plastics Works."

Hector speaks up. "Maybe we can get our own aerial photograph."

Malik snorts. "You got a pet hawk I don't know about?"

Hector makes a face at him. "Go fly a kite."

* * *

Here's a tip: never let boys into your studio. They're all thumbs.

The thin wooden dowel snaps in Malik's hand when I ask him to hold it; Hector pours quick-drying glue on his shoes; Eli can't cut through a two-ply plastic garbage bag without shredding it. I end up doing everything myself while those three clods stare at me like I'm spinning straw into gold.

I'm just wrapping the plastic around the frame of the kite to make the sail when I spy Amber outside my house. "Get down!" I hiss.

"Why?" asks Malik. "So we're here? So what?"

"I've been ducking her to work on our plans," I explain breathlessly. "You want me to have to explain that?"

We sit on the floor away from the window, crouching low as I finish the sail. The doorbell rings . . . once . . . twice. My parents aren't home so nobody answers.

Eventually, I spy Amber through the window, walking away.

"The coast is clear," I announce, suddenly feeling like a lousy friend.

The day is sunny and blustery—at least, blustery for around here. Sometimes the prevailing winds are pushed south toward us by the mountains of Colorado. Of course, that information comes from school, so it isn't necessarily true. For all we know, some mythological wind god blows over Serenity through titanic lips.

But today nobody's complaining. We've got good visibility and enough wind to keep the kite in the air.

I squint up at it, using a hand to shield my eyes from the bright sun. "Do you think we got what we need?"

Eli lets out more string, his hands working deftly on the spool. I built the kite, but he added the most important part—a small wireless webcam fastened to the diamond frame. "Let's go a little higher. The camera's pointing straight down. So unless we're directly over the factory, we could miss it."

"If the kite's too far up, we might not be able to see anything," Hector warns.

Eli is unconcerned. "The camera's pretty high-res, so we can zoom in without too much loss of sharpness."

It's all Greek to me. Eli's the tech guy. I'm just the kite-maker.

"As your doctor," comes a deep, sarcastic voice, "it's my medical opinion that flying a kite from the middle of a public street can be hazardous to your health."

We wheel. It's Dr. Bruder, beaming over a red bow tie,

amused (and maybe a little too curious?).

"Right, Dad," Malik replies. "Like the traffic's really heavy today. If we're still here at rush hour, we might even see a car."

"It only takes one. Or one of the trucks from the factory. I don't see why you have to be here. There's plenty of open space at the park."

We started in the park. The wind kept taking the kite (and the webcam) away from the Plastics Works. Aerial photographs of the rocks outside of town might look beautiful in my studio, but they're not going to show us the roof of the factory.

Obviously, that isn't an explanation we can give Dr. Bruder.

We're all tongue-tied, and it crosses my mind that this is more dangerous than it appears to be on the surface. If the adults suspect that something's up (even if they can't figure out what) they might start watching us a little more closely. You don't have much chance of breaking into a factory if you can't make it past your own front door.

Hector bails us out. "Too many trees at the park. Our kite kept getting tangled in branches."

It sounds so reasonable we almost believe it ourselves.

"I suppose," Dr. Bruder concedes. "But cars could

come at any time, so please be careful." And he's on his way.

"Nice save," Malik compliments Hector once the coast is clear. "Don't let me catch you lying to *me* like that."

"Don't worry," Hector grins. "If it happens, you'll never know."

I peer up at the kite, which flutters above the tallest of the smokestacks. "Surely we've got a good picture by now."

Eli begins to reel in the line. "We'll find out tonight."

"Tonight?" Malik echoes. "Why not now?"

"I set the camera to upload to a website," Eli explains, still winding. "That's on the real internet, not the watered-down bag of lies we get here. We'll have to check it from the factory grounds."

I brace myself for another midnight sneak-out.

I'm almost late. Steve gets wrapped up in a West Coast baseball game that goes into extra innings. Until someone finally scores, I'm trapped in my room, with my arms wrapped around my knees, rocking and waiting. This whole thing is completely freaking me out.

I make it, though, and meet Eli under the big maple tree. Malik and Hector, who are neighbors, arrive together, bickering about something, but quietly.

"Ready for round two?" Eli asks.

We retrace our steps toward the Plastics Works. It's even scarier this time around, because we know there are Purples prowling the grounds.

Then we get a break. As we approach the base of the Fellowship hill, Eli's iPad suddenly picks up a faint Wi-Fi signal from the Plastics Works. This is huge. It means we'll be able to get the real internet without having to trespass on factory grounds. We duck into some tall grass just outside the perimeter fence and crowd around Eli.

Something bothers me. "If the town went to all the trouble to create a fake internet, it's because they don't want us to see the real thing, right? So how come they didn't make it harder to find?"

Hector has a theory. "If the real Wi-Fi works in the factory and the fake Wi-Fi works in our houses, maybe no one thought to check where one stops and the other starts."

"Figures," Malik mumbles. "It's like buying three giant trucks and driving them all over the place, but never bothering to dust off the cones so they'll look new."

"We need to remember that," Eli puts in. "The people

we're up against aren't always as thorough as they could be."

"'The people we're up against'?" Malik challenges. "Why can't you admit the truth? Those 'people' are our own parents."

"Not necessarily everybody," I say, tight-lipped.

"Dream on, Torific—"

"I've got it," Eli announces suddenly, his fingers just a blur on his iPad's touch screen.

He holds the tablet out to us. I squint at what appears to be a series of black-and-white images of town. There are big beautiful homes, kidney-shaped and rectangular pools, immaculate landscaping. How could anything be wrong in such a perfect place?

Now we know it's only perfect from the air.

Hector indicates the top of the screen, which reads *Ohio Lollipop Festival*. "Why is it called that?"

Eli shrugs. "I figured our parents might be checking the internet for anything about the Serenity Plastics Works. But no way will they be looking out for a lollipop festival."

(There it is again—our parents as the enemy.)

Malik is unimpressed. "These may as well be pictures

of lollipops if they don't show us a way into the factory. Can you see anything? I sure can't."

Eli manipulates the screen. "Let me get us a better view." He selects the clearest of the images and zooms in on the roof.

From above, the Plastics Works resembles a gigantic rectangular birthday cake with grainy gray icing and three smokestack candles.

Hector points. "What's that dark part over there?"

We lean in.

"It looks like a separate section," Malik notes, "walled off from the rest of the roof."

Hector frowns. "Not separate, *lower*. See? It's in the shadow of the rest of the building."

"Like a halfway point!" I exclaim. "We can use it as a stepping-stone—climb from the ground to there, and then from there to the roof."

"But how do we get inside?" asks Eli.

Malik's brow furrows. "There must be roof access. You know, so if the air-conditioning breaks, they don't have to hoist the repair guy up by crane."

And then I have it. "See that dark square underneath the compressor? I think it's a trapdoor. That could be our way in."

"Could be?" Malik challenges. "I'm not a big fan of climbing giant buildings for nothing."

"I know it's risky," Eli decides. "But the choice is between doing this and doing nothing. And doing nothing isn't an option."

13

MALIK BRUDER

My greatest fear used to be that I'd be stuck in Happy Valley forever, busting my butt at some dead-end job at the plastics factory.

But that's been looking better to me lately. Steady job, steady pay, no falling off roofs and scrambling your brains on the ground below.

And now I can't even look forward to that. The factory is as screwy as the town, and instead of working in it, I'll be invading the place.

The time is set: Tuesday, 1:00 a.m.

I'm not the only one who's nervous. Frieden says he can't sleep. Little Miss Torific has been having nightmares about her parents in Purple People Eater outfits. It's pretty funny, but dark circles under her eyes confirm that bad dreams have been keeping her up at night. Hector keeps telling me how calm he is, and the fact that he won't shut up about it says exactly the opposite. The poor wimp is so afraid of being left out that he signed on to this without a sensible thought. Maybe he really is "special."

What freaks me out most of all is the part we won't be able to know until we're face-to-face with it: What's inside the factory? Is it crawling with Purples? And if they aren't making traffic cones, what *are* they doing? I want to know, but I'm afraid of what I might find out.

And there's one other thing I'll bet none of the others has considered. What if we break in and discover . . . nothing? No explanation of "something screwy," but also nothing to put our minds to rest?

If that happens, I think I'll lose it for sure.

9:25 p.m. A geyser of water explodes from the kitchen faucet, striking my dad full in the chest, just below the bow tie. He drops like a sack of flour, and the jet shoots across the room, soaking the microwave, which shorts out in a shower of sparks.

All I can think is why tonight? Nothing ever happens in Happy Valley, and our sink has to turn into Niagara Falls *the one night we've got something going on!*

Miraculously, the house is not burning down, but it might as well be, if you go by my mother's reaction. "Malik, get Peter Amani! Henry, shut the water off before the kitchen is flooded!"

It's a little late for that. We're already up to our ankles. To be honest, I don't care if the house floats downstream to Arizona and ends up in the Colorado River. My concern is the plan. I want a calm evening, everything nice and dull. The last thing we need is a crisis with my parents and Hector's dad up in the air, frantic and possibly sleepless.

The Amanis live two doors away, so I run over there, rather than calling. It's easier to ignore a ringing telephone than someone pounding on the door screaming, "Flood!"

Hector answers the door, and I bark, "Get your dad! We've got a plumbing emergency!"

He stares at me. "*Tonight?*"

"Yeah, I did it on purpose just to tick you off! *Hurry!*"

Soon, Mr. Amani is on his way, with Hector and me bringing up the rear. The word around Happy Valley is that Hector's dad breaks as many pipes as he repairs, but he *is* the only plumber in town—also electrician and general handyman. If he can't fix it, you're looking at Taos. I breathe a silent prayer as he splashes into our kitchen, wielding a very destructive-looking wrench. My father's there to greet him. Dad's put on a dry bow tie for the crisis, like that's what it says in Plumbing 101.

"I hope you've brought your scuba gear, Pete." Dad's jokes aren't just for the kids in town. He's an equal opportunity doofus.

Hearts sinking as the water level rises, Hector and I watch Mr. Amani get to work.

"What if it's a long job?" Hector worries in a whisper.

"It won't be," I say firmly. There's absolutely no basis in fact for my opinion. It's strictly hope.

"Yeah, but what I mean is—"

"I *know* what you mean, stupid! And if you don't shut up, *everyone's* going to know!"

It's after eleven by the time the sink is fixed. That turns out to be the easy part. Cleaning up the water is a lot harder. Hector and I drag over these big drying fans, which have to run for twenty-four hours. Each one sounds like a leaf blower with a large stone rattling around inside it. I figure we'll have to scrap the mission. No way are my parents going to be able to sleep through that racket. It's enough to wake the dead.

Hector shares my concern. He lingers even after his father has headed home. "What are we going to *do*?"

147

I think it over, the fans roaring in my ears. Tonight is a big deal—not just putting together the plan, but also getting ourselves psyched up to *do* it. If we cancel now, who knows how long it'll take to get ourselves to recharge again.

"It's almost eleven thirty," I tell him. "If my folks aren't asleep by midnight, we call everything off. You'll just go to the meeting place and tell Eli and Tori."

"Why me?"

"Because if I could do it, there'd be no reason to cancel, would there?"

Miracle of miracles, both my parents are dead to the world within twenty minutes of crawling into bed. Go figure. Those fans are so droning and monotonous that I almost drop off myself. Wouldn't that be classic—to snooze through my own break-in?

I don't even have to tiptoe as I slip out of the house. My folks wouldn't hear it if I left on horseback at the head of a brass band.

The drill is becoming familiar: meet Hector first, then Eli and Tori. She's brought ropes, courtesy of Mr. Pritel, who used to be a rock climber. Then on to the factory.

I'm waiting my turn to scale the gate when Hector freezes halfway up.

"Sometime tonight would be nice," I stage-whisper. "What's the problem?"

"My pants are stuck," he calls down.

"Get them *unstuck!*" I hiss.

He flounders. "I can't!"

Muttering under my breath, I climb the fence to Hector, and Eli and Tori, who are already over, clamber up the other side. Hector's right—he really *is* caught. Somehow, a strand of chain link pierced the denim of his jeans, and all his efforts to free himself only tangled him even further.

"Take off your pants," Tori orders.

He's horrified. "I'm not breaking into the factory in my underwear!"

"It'll be easier to get them off the fence if you're not in them," she explains. "Obviously, you'll put them on again afterward."

"Like it matters what we're wearing if the Purples bust us," I add, rolling my eyes.

Hector sets his jaw. "No."

"What do you mean no?" I demand. "What choice is there?"

Hector points at Tori. "Not with *her* watching."

She eases herself down a few handholds and jumps to

the ground. "How's this?" she asks, turning her back.

She's the best climber of the four of us, and we could probably use her help. But after much protesting and whining Eli and I manage to get Hector separated from his jeans and over the gate. At least he has the grace to look embarrassed as he gets dressed again. It's comic relief, but it's also a reminder: Things can—and do—go wrong.

At last, we approach the building. It looks different from our first visit. Higher.

"Ready, you guys?" whispers Tori, all business.

I don't think I'll ever be ready, and Eli and Hector are scared witless. But a strange calm seems to set in with Tori the closer we get to crunch time.

Step 1. Time the Purples. A circuit of the building takes the golf cart twenty-one minutes. To be safe, we allow ourselves eighteen for the first stage of our climb.

The instant the patrol disappears out of sight, we steal along the wall and position ourselves directly under the lower section of roof that we chose from the aerial photographs. It's still easily twenty feet up, maybe more.

Step 2. Cowboy time. I tie a wide noose at the end of the rope, take aim, and hurl the loop at the roof. The first few tries aren't high enough, but then I get the range. The snare disappears over the edge, only to miss its target and fall back down at my feet.

I'm shooting for a hook-shaped vent pipe we spotted on the kite pictures. It's just a few inches in from the eave, but from twenty feet down and blocked by the angle of the roof, I'm working blind.

"Eight minutes," Tori supplies the time check.

"Think you can do better?" I growl.

"I'd be more on target," she replies honestly. "But I don't have the strength to throw high enough."

It's a little more Happy Valley honesty than I'm in the mood for.

The nylon cord is growing heavy in my hands. It's like I'm carrying an anvil. I start to sweat. My shoulders ache.

"Twelve minutes," Tori chimes.

Okay, now I'm worried. Remember, it's not enough just to hook the pipe. Four people have to climb the rope and pull it out of sight before the Purples come around again.

"We don't have much time!" Hector intones urgently.

I glare at him, and the tiny pause is just the rest my tired arm needs. On the next throw, the rope doesn't come back. I pull it taut and it holds.

"Fifteen minutes," Hector updates us.

Tori hoists herself off the ground and climbs with

ease, "walking" along the bricks. I have to admit she's good—better than I'll probably be. At the top, she swings a leg over the eave and disappears from sight. A second later, she's leaning out, calling for the next climber.

It's Eli, shinnying madly up the rope, propelled by fear rather than athleticism. He doesn't earn many style points, but he gets up almost as quickly. After him comes Hector. With no chain link to shish kebab himself on, the shrimp does okay—at least until he reaches the top, where he struggles to get his foot over the ledge.

"Hurry, Hector! We're at eighteen minutes!" Tori hisses.

To underscore this point, we hear the hum of the golf cart in the distance, growing louder. Oh no! The Purples are making it in record time.

Eli and Tori reach down and haul Hector in like fishermen landing a prize tarpon. Then they pull up the rope. Tori rasps a single syllable: "Hide!"

There's nowhere to go. The bushes are too far away and the patrol is too close. The golf cart's wheels churn against the ground. They're about to turn the corner. And what will they find? Me, serving myself up on a silver platter.

I don't know what makes me do it. I just do. I lie flat

on the grass against the foot of the building and try to melt into the ground.

There is absolutely no cover. If the Purples glance in my direction, I'm hosed.

The flashlight beams appear first, crisscrossing the compound the way they always do. Here comes the golf cart, less than ten feet away. Their faces are as clear as their pictures on the cards—General Confusion and Alexander the Grape. A cone of light shoots straight at me, sweeps across my shoulders, lights up my nose . . .

. . . and moves on! I lie there, frozen with fear, waiting for the patrol to come back and scoop me up. Instead, they drive past. I'm a statue. I don't even breathe as the cart rolls off into the night.

Finally, a voice from above: "Clear."

I barely hear Eli over the pounding of my heart in my ears. Why didn't they see me? I was right there, like, in a spotlight. It must honestly be true that you don't notice what you're not expecting to see.

Down comes the rope and I climb up to join the others. I make pretty short work of it, too, riding an adrenaline rush that could just as easily have taken me to the moon.

It's time for Step 3, which is no small thing for a guy who didn't expect to survive Step 2. We pull up the rope again, and I take aim at the main roof. It's a trickier throw this time, practically vertical, since I can't stand back for a better angle without tumbling off the level I'm already on. Amazingly, I make it on the third try, and we prepare for our final ascent. It's only another twenty feet, but it feels like a mile in the sky.

"Don't think about how far down the ground is," Tori advises. "Remember, if you slip, you'll just fall back to where we are now."

"Or this is where we'll bounce," I mutter, "on our way to being dashed to pieces at the bottom."

"Sounds like something your dad might say," Hector jabs at me.

I'm too stressed out to be insulted.

Tori goes first, her strong hands working the cord as her sneakers scamper lightly up the husk of the building. I'm amazed at how athletic she is. Then again, when the only things you ever try are badminton, water polo, and croquet, who knows what hidden talents could be lurking just beneath the surface.

She's almost at the top when it happens. With barely a sound, the noose slips off its purchase on the roof. For a terrible instant, I see the loose rope above us, unhinged from the factory. Then it's falling, and so is Tori.

She thrashes around desperately as she lets go of the useless rope. I hold out both arms, which is stupid—she's eighteen feet up, so catching her isn't an option. Or maybe that's my secret plan—if I get crushed, I won't have to face the prospect of getting down off the building carrying a dead body.

I hear twin gasps from Eli and Hector and brace for impact.

Tori's flailing right hand catches the small ledge at the bottom of a window. Grimacing with effort, she holds on, digging the rubber toes of her sneakers into the space between the bricks.

She'll never make it, I think to myself. But somehow, she does, sticking to the wall as if by Velcro. The rope lands at my feet.

I pick it up and start flinging it at the roof, hoping to hook something quickly, to give Tori an easy way up. Or down. At this point, I don't care about our mission; I just don't want anybody dead. Again and again, the snare misses its target and tumbles back to my level.

"Look!" Eli whispers.

It's Tori—*moving* on the wall! She stretches with her left hand and jams it between bricks, finding just enough leverage to hoist her feet to the window ledge. From there, she can reach the eaves. She heaves herself up with both arms and rolls over onto the roof. I experience a twinge of fear as she disappears from sight. Then she's back in view, on her feet and signaling me to toss her the rope. She catches it and loops it around a sturdy pipe.

One by one, we clamber up the wall and huddle together at the top, exhausted and speechless.

"You okay?" I breathe.

She manages a weak nod. "Thanks, Malik." At that, she looks better than Eli and Hector, who are grim, pale, and hyperventilating. I don't have a mirror, but I'm sure I'm worse. I can barely keep myself from shaking.

We're on the roof of the Serenity Plastics Works—the highest point of our universe for our entire lives. Every time you look up, there it is.

Eli puts it into words. "This must be how it felt to stand on the summit of Mount Everest for the first time."

"If there *is* a Mount Everest," I remind him. "We learned about it in school, so it might be total baloney."

From our perch, Serenity seems every bit the tiny Podunk I've always known it to be. Take away a few streetlights and you wouldn't even know there's a town.

The seesawing beams of the patrol pass below us, and

we retreat from the edge of the roof. Our shoes crunch on the gravelly surface.

Besides the smokestacks, the largest feature up here is the massive air-conditioning unit, located near the center of the roof. We head for it, wending our way around various pipes and vents. We have to find the trapdoor we saw in the aerial photograph.

There it is, in the shadow of the big compressor. I grab the handle and pull. It won't budge.

Tori takes a flat butter knife from her pocket, and slips the blade into the crack between the square door and the frame, feeling for the latch. "I've been practicing on our door at home." She makes a face. "It isn't quite the same." She twists harder, and we hear the snap. When she withdraws the knife, half the blade is missing.

She looks so crestfallen that it begins to sink in that nobody thought to bring any other equipment to gain access to the building. This is classic—we've risked our necks and come so far, and it turns out that our entire plan hinges on a *butter knife*?

"That's all we have to get inside?" I exclaim, barely able to keep myself from shouting. *"That?"*

Even in the gloom I can see her redden. "I learned on

the locks in my house—"

"And it never occurred to you that all locks aren't the same as the ones in a place where *nobody locks anything?*" I scoop up a fistful of gravel, squeezing until the pain of my hand matches the agony in my gut. I rear back and let fly with maximum frustration and rage. A few pebbles strike the corner of the air-conditioning unit with a rat-a-tat sound.

"Cut it out!" Eli hisses. "What if the patrol hears us?"

"They're forty feet below us."

"It *was* pretty loud," Hector ventures.

Tori jumps up excitedly. "You're right! It *was* loud!"

"So?" I sputter.

"So it was loud because the metal is *hollow!* The air-conditioning is a duct system through the whole building!"

"And I care about this because . . . ?"

"Don't you see?" she exclaims. "The trapdoor isn't the only way into the factory! The air ducts go in too! And we go in with them!"

14

HECTOR AMANI

I know what people sometimes think of me: too young. Too small. Too clumsy. Too chicken.

Well, I may be some of those other things, but I'm *not* chicken. When Malik removes the access panel to the ventilation system, he practically loses his dinner at the prospect of going down that narrow, dark shaft. He doesn't think I know he has claustrophobia—or maybe it's just the fact that he has a big behind and he doesn't like to get it squeezed into tight places.

Tori takes a small flashlight out of her pocket and shines it into the opening. The shaft heads straight down about seven or eight feet before splitting off in different directions. "Somebody will have to stay on the roof to lower the others down by rope."

"I'll do it," Malik volunteers immediately.

"Fine," I tell him. "I'll go in."

"You?" Malik brays a laugh. "You can't even ride a bike!"

Eli looks skeptical. "I don't know, Hector. Maybe you'd be better off staying up here just in case Malik needs any—uh—help."

"It's going to be a tight squeeze in the ducts, and I'm the smallest."

The plan is set. Malik waits up top to get us in and out, and the rest of us tackle the factory.

I squeeze that cord until my hands burn as Malik lowers me into the ventilation system, leering at me all the way down. He knows how scared I am, and I'm not going to give him the satisfaction of being right. The others didn't pick me to be part of this group; I had to sneak my way in. But now that I'm here, I'm going to prove that I can get the job done as well as anybody. Even if we don't understand exactly what that job is supposed to be.

I feel a mixture of triumph and dread when my feet touch the bottom. I drop to my knees and crawl along the passage to my left. The instant I'm surrounded by tin, the isolation is total, and I'd give anything for one last glimpse of Malik's trademark smirk.

Eli lands next, and quickly folds himself out of the way to make room for Tori. We're like a long caterpillar, with me at the head and Tori bringing up the rear, wriggling along the channel. We seem to be on a level course. I get the sense that the ductwork must be directly under the building ceiling, but it's impossible to be sure. All we can see in Tori's flashlight beam is the dull silver tunnel.

Then my groping hand strikes a different texture— not the dusty smoothness of the tin, but a rough metal grid. My weight knocks it loose, and it's falling. At the last second, I reach out and grab it, and suddenly, I'm falling too.

Terror blurs my vision, but I do glimpse a vast factory floor in the gloom of half-light. Part of me understands this information is useless to me. In a matter of a few violent seconds, I'll be on that floor, broken and dead.

Illogically, my last thought is not of my parents. It's of Malik, who's going to miss me, even though he might not admit it.

Strong hands grab my ankles, and Eli is yanking me back into the duct. I bring the grate up with me and fit it into place.

I try to quaver "Thanks!" but no sound comes out. I scramble past the opening and Eli and Tori inch up and peer through the grille.

Eli whistles. "Man, Hector! You could have died!"

A brave and clever response dies in my throat. My mouth is still not working.

Safe for the moment, we stare down at the factory floor.

I see the orange first. Cones—a lot of them. At least a few hundred—freestanding, stacked on pallets, and piled in a mound.

Okay, I tell myself, still not thinking 100 percent clearly. *We broke into a traffic cone plant and found traffic cones. What did we expect?*

"Were we wrong about this place?" breathes Tori.

Eli is shaking his head. Is the factory exactly what it's supposed to be?

Then my head clears and I realize what I *don't* see. Equipment. Machinery. What made all this? And out of what? There's no raw material either. I expand my view. Four high brick walls with very few windows; a concrete floor painted battleship gray. A forklift, several folding tables, a riding lawn mower; beside that, a small stepladder that would reach about 3 percent of the way to the ceiling. There's a lunchroom area in the far corner. A vast shelving unit, largely empty, except for the occasional flashlight or coil of twine, and, for some reason, a lamp shade with no lamp. That's about it.

"No way," I tell the other two. "This isn't a factory, it's a front for a factory. If they're making cones, they're doing it with a magic wand."

Eli nods. "No machines."

"And no plastic either," I add. "How can you have a plastics factory without plastic?"

Tori's voice is shaky. "What do my parents do all day in this place?"

"This whole plant is a cover," Eli concludes, stone-faced.

It's a big discovery, but our reaction is muted. Not shock. It's sort of a relief, I guess—relief that we're not crazy. Still, there's so much we don't know.

"But if it *is* a cover," I ask, picturing my mother painstakingly assembling her bag lunch to come to this un-factory, "what are they covering?"

None of us has an answer for that.

Tori peers sideways through the angled grille of the grating. "That wall," she says, "is too close."

I'm confused. "Where would you like it to be?"

"This duct should end where the factory does." She indicates the passage ahead of us. "But look—it goes on at least another forty feet. Which means—"

Eli clues in. "There's something behind those bricks. A whole other part of the building."

"And we're heading straight for it," adds Tori.

We resume our caterpillar motion. I'm still in the lead, crawling carefully around other gratings. One of them is just a few feet in front of the mysterious wall. So we have a pretty good idea when we've left the open plant and entered the hidden section.

Thirty feet ahead of us, a square of light beckons. I'm guessing it's some kind of room, since it's brighter than the dim factory we've just come from.

A minute later I'm peering down at a regular office— a desk in front of a bank of TV monitors. Although the screens are lit and running, the chair is empty.

"What is it?" Tori whispers behind me.

I squeeze past the opening to give her and Eli a peek. "Some kind of security station. But nobody's there."

Eli frowns through the grille. "Security for a factory that doesn't make anything?"

Tori gives it her practiced eye. "It's no more than a five- or six-foot drop to that desk. I'm going in."

"I'm with you." Eli pushes out the grating, angles it, and draws it up inside the duct.

"Wait," I protest in a low voice. "That chair isn't there for decoration, you know. A butt goes in it, probably a purple one. What'll we do if the guy comes back?"

Neither of them considers my question worthy of an answer. Before I know it, Tori is through the opening and lowering herself toward the tabletop. When she drops, it's only a couple of feet to the desk. For Eli, who's taller, it's even less.

Once more I'm on the outside looking in—although, technically, I'm on the inside looking out. "Should I stay up here? You know, to help you guys back up? Yeah, that's probably a good idea . . ."

But then they start having a fit over what's on the monitors.

"What is it?" I crane my neck out of the ceiling, and before I know it, I'm falling again. Floundering, I grab the frame of the duct opening and jump down to the desk. It's not as clean a landing as theirs. I bounce off, hit the carpet, and roll. Not exactly Olympic gymnast stuff, but at least I don't knock myself unconscious.

There are eighteen screens, each one showing a live feed from some part of Serenity. There's the schoolyard, Dr. Bruder's office, the general store, and the restaurant. There's the park, and a close-up on the Serenity Cup.

"No wonder they don't lock the case," Eli comments. "The instant someone lays a finger on that thing, they'll know."

There are several views of town streets, as well as two shots of Old County Six—one to the west of Serenity and one to the east. One image seems to be out in an area of sagebrush. Spotlights illuminate a large helicopter parked on a concrete pad. There are two Purple People Eaters in the picture. One is Baron Vladimir von Horseteeth. The other I don't recognize—he might have been hired after Eli and Randy made the cards.

The reality sinks in for all three of us.

"They've got cameras everywhere!" I whisper. "They're spying on us!"

Eli draws a nervous breath. "It's a miracle we haven't been spotted sneaking out to the factory. Look—they've got one on the front door but nothing on the gate."

"What about our route through town?" I wonder.

Tori's gaze moves methodically from screen to screen. You can almost see her putting together a picture of Serenity with the cameras superimposed on it. "Pure luck," she concludes. "We haven't tripped any of their surveillance."

"We have to retrace our steps exactly," I add anxiously.

"In fact, we should probably start right now—"

"Not until we check out *that*," says Eli.

He's pointing to an opening in the floor ringed by a wrought-iron railing. It's a tight spiral staircase winding down to another level.

"What about the guy from that chair?" I protest.

Tori sneaks a glance over the rail. "I don't see anybody. Let's go."

I follow them, mostly because I'm too scared to stay in the room by myself. Even when we tiptoe, our footfalls on the iron steps reverberate with a gonglike sound.

Downstairs, we step off into what seems to be some kind of publishing office. A large printing press dominates the center of the room. Eli nudges a computer mouse, and the machine's large monitor comes out of hibernation. The display shows the front page of the *Pax*, dateline: tomorrow. The headline reads:

SERENITY VOTED #1 IN NEW MEXICO
FOR QUALITY OF LIFE
UNPRECEDENTED 14TH STRAIGHT YEAR

Eli snorts. "They ought to know how great it is. They're watching every inch of the place."

There are always a few national and international news stories in the *Pax*, and now we know where they come from. The front pages from several well-known papers are up on two huge touch screens—the *New York Times*, the *Washington Post*, the *Wall Street Journal*, and a few others. Some of the stories have been highlighted, others deselected in gray.

For example, in the *Los Angeles Times*, *Two Dead in Gang Shootout* has been nixed, but the piece directly above it, *Celebrity Flower Show Opens*, has been left intact. On the next screen, where the *Times* of London is displayed, *Terrorist Bombing Rocks Mayfair* has been cut. However, *Buckingham Palace to Get Spring Cleaning* is totally okay.

"This is how the *Pax* chooses what to print?" I whisper in awe. "By taking out any bad news?"

Eli nods. "They do it to the internet too. No Revolutionary War, just tea."

"But we learn about wars too," Tori reasons. "And crime."

"Only as an example, to show how much better things are here," Eli explains. "The Boston Tea Party was a rebellion. Think about the Essential Qualities—honesty, harmony, contentment. Nothing about questioning authority, or fighting for your rights."

"All the more reason we should get out of here before anybody catches us rebelling!" I beg.

Tori points toward the spiral staircase. "There's another level below us. Didn't you see it?"

"We're pushing our luck!"

But Eli and Tori are already tiptoeing that way.

I'm getting really scared, but I follow them to what seems to be the bottom floor. At least, this is where the steps end. It's a large circular conference room, dimly lit. The rounded walls are made almost entirely of whiteboard material. These are covered in photographs and note cards, hundreds—no, thousands of them, pinned up by small magnets.

Tori shines her light on a section of the wall.

The shock begins in the base of my spine and works its way northward until I hear a buzzing in my ears.

It's *me*.

My first baby pictures, toddler shots, photographs of me at every age, right up to this year's school portrait. Some of the prints and notes are faded, curled, and yellow with age. At the top of the board is a large label, spelled out in block capitals:

HECTOR AMANI

BORN: 02/15/2003

Osiris?

It's my whole life, documented in detail—how much I weighed at birth. How long my mother was pregnant with me. There's a picture of her as a younger woman, feeding me in a high chair, and a high-angle shot of our classroom that seems to show me angling my test paper into Malik's field of vision. There must be hidden cameras at school!

More: my academic records, behavior charts, results of medical tests. *Brain Scan, 7/29/2005*; I had a brain scan? There are medical printouts and graphs I can't even begin to understand. Notes scribbled in my parents' handwriting, Mr. Frieden's, Dr. Bruder's, Mrs. Laska's . . . *stratospheric IQ . . . exceptional reasoning skills . . . emotionally immature . . . socially awkward . . . vulnerable to intimidation . . . Incident report: subject took extra brownie . . .* Extra brownie? Are they serious?

There are dozens of these reports, maybe hundreds. *Subject failed to reveal unfair advantage in recreational test* . . . It's dated Serenity Day, 2011. Has everything I've ever done been under a microscope? And why are they calling me "subject"?

The beam swings away, and I'm left staring at the darkened wall. "Hey, I was reading that!"

"Oh my God!" exclaims Tori in a hoarse whisper. "It's me! And you, Eli!"

She pans the wall. Eleven Serenity kids are chronicled in vast collages of pictures, papers, and notes. Each display is just as thorough as mine. Amber is there as well. She's Osiris 6. And also Malik, Osiris 3. Eli has the top spot—Osiris 1, whatever that means. But there's no Randy, no Stanley Cole, no Melanie Brandt, no Fowler twins.

"How come not everybody's here?" I wonder.

Eli's voice is strangled as he quotes from Randy's letter. "Some of us are *special*." He takes out his iPad and circles the room, meticulously photographing every whiteboard, and the long conference table, which is covered with papers.

I don't feel special. I feel violated, invaded, and extremely creeped out. I feel like I'm some kind of lab rat!

Tori is visibly upset. "Don't try to make sense of this! None of this makes any sense! I'm supposed to be Osiris

9! It's on notes signed by my own parents! What's an Osiris?"

I'm so gobsmacked that I've forgotten where I am and what I'm doing. At that moment, my mind is a boiling whirlwind of questions. One question, really: *Why?* Why have eleven kids been studied since the minute they were born?

That's when we hear footsteps gonging on the spiral staircase two flights up, and the fear returns in a skipped heartbeat. The purple butt that fits in the video station chair is on its way down.

I look around in desperation. A single door leads to the main factory area. Eli beats me to it, so he gets the bad news first: locked.

We can make out the jingling of keys now, and a gruff voice humming a tuneless melody. It's like all the worst-case scenarios rolled into one. In a few seconds, he'll be upon us, and we've got no escape.

Eli and I stand there, looking helplessly at each other. His eyes flicker toward the conference table—the only available hiding place. But it has a glass top, so the guard would have to be blind and stupid not to notice us hunkered down underneath it.

I'm coming to terms with the fact that my life is about

to change in a fundamental way, and not one I think I'm going to enjoy. My mind reels. Is there a way out of this—?

"Over here!" Tori hisses in a barely audible voice.

She's squatting at the wall beside an air-conditioning register. The grate is off, and she's motioning us into the duct.

I'm so frozen that Eli practically has to drag me. He crawls into the opening, pulling me after him. Tori scrambles in last, crushing my legs, and replaces the grille behind her. Through the grid, I see boots topped with purple cuffs on the tile of the conference room. That's how close it is. Another couple of seconds and we would have been too late. We're out and he's in, almost in the same instant.

We cower there, listening to him clearing his throat. We don't even breathe, much less move. If he hears us, we're cooked.

The boots issue a sharp report—*crack!*—with every step on the tile floor. I feel each one inside my skull, a series of jarring knocks against my brain. But—

Are the footsteps becoming quieter? I peer through the grating. *The guard is walking away from us!*

With her finger, Tori gestures above us. At first, I don't understand. And when I finally do, I wish I didn't.

The duct we're in is an offshoot of the ventilation line we crawled across on. It is plumb-line vertical. In other words, the only way out of here is by climbing straight up through a featureless metal tunnel without so much as a single handhold. And we have to do it silently, to avoid attracting the attention of the Purple People Eater on the other side of the wall.

Above me, Eli presses the rubber soles of his shoes into the sides of the tin passage and lifts himself a few inches, pushing outward with his hands to jam himself in so he doesn't fall.

"I can't do it," I whisper. But I have to be so quiet that my words don't reach the others.

Tori is already shoving me from below.

I try to say no, but I don't dare produce any sound. I realize in horror that I'm going to have to do the impossible because there's no way to refuse without giving away our presence in the duct.

It's the most grueling, exhausting, painful, and unpleasant thing I've ever attempted. Once we've made it a few feet up from the bottom, warm, slimy droplets begin to rain on me—Eli's sweat. I realize that I, in turn, am sweating all over Tori, who deserves better. Not only is she climbing herself, but she's boosting me ahead of her.

About ten feet up, we reach the print shop level. Gingerly, Eli eases the grating out of the wall.

"Did you catch that Dodgers game last night?" comes an adult voice.

A flash of purple fabric passes by the opening. *A second guard!*

Eli is so startled that he drops the grating to the tiles. In that instant, the entire world grinds to a halt as we freeze inside the duct. If they heard us . . .

"Yeah, a real pitcher's duel. It all came down to that squeeze play in the bottom of the seventh . . ."

Three kids have never been so perfectly still and soundless. Somehow, in their baseball conversation, the Purples missed the clatter of the grating. Miracle.

Carefully, Eli fits the register back into place and we climb on, an inch at a time. I'm getting better at this, but not much. The agony in my shoulders is excruciating, and the effort to keep my sneakers jammed against the sides feels as if I'm being torn in two, like a wishbone. It's an unimaginable ordeal when you can't allow yourself so much as the luxury of a groan.

Eli passes the outlet for the surveillance monitoring station. He doesn't even consider exiting there—not with two Purples on the scene.

Still ten feet to the top. A new worry begins to nag at me. We're now high enough that if Eli slips, he'll wipe us all out permanently. It's a very long way down, the equivalent of a three-story building. And it's only becoming longer.

I can tell when Eli sees the end in sight. He speeds up, if you can use the word *speed* to describe our snail-like progress. Whimpering with exertion, he hauls himself into the main passage and reaches down to help me. I swear this is the scariest part—to be so close, with the danger of falling still very much a possibility. The walls are slick with perspiration and my body is a single blinding ache.

And then I'm there, lying flat on my face on the cool metal. Never could I have imagined that simply being horizontal could feel so glorious. I can't move; Tori has to climb over me, digging her sneakers into my back. I barely notice. There are degrees of pain, and this one barely registers after what we've just gone through.

Gonging footsteps on the metal stairs indicate that the Purples are on their way up. I grasp the problem immediately, but Eli and Tori haven't figured it out yet. And there's no way I can warn them—not with the guards so close.

I squeeze past them in the tiny space. The next time Malik calls me shrimp, I intend to tell him about this moment. No way could somebody his size have managed it.

There it is in the duct ahead of me—the grating we removed to climb down to the security station. If the Purples happen to look up, they're going to see a hole in the ceiling where the grille is supposed to be!

The gonging sound is very close now. *They must be right at the top of the stairs!* I can't risk crawling—it would make too much noise. In desperation, I launch myself forward, belly-sliding along the passage. Without stopping, I snatch up the grating, reach it down through the opening, and then pull it back into position, just as the two Purples appear at the top of the stairs below me.

One by one, we slither noiselessly over the security station, clutching our guts during those terrifying seconds we spend exposed, directly above the guards. Once we're past, though, moving forward, instead of up, it seems as easy as a stroll down Fellowship Avenue. We cross over the factory floor and soon reach the main feed from the air conditioner on the roof.

That first glimpse of night sky is the most beautiful sight I've ever laid eyes on. Then it's gone, and Malik's big ugly mug is blocking the view. Actually, he looks beautiful too. Anybody would.

"What took you so long?" he rasps.

"Not now," Eli groans. "Get us out of here!"

Malik drops the rope down to us, and we climb up to the roof. The second my feet hit the gravel, my legs collapse under me, and I sit there, cross-legged, weeping.

"Are you guys all right?" asks Malik. He seems pretty frazzled himself. It couldn't have been easy, waiting up here all alone, wondering what he would do if we didn't come back.

"I'm not sure any of us are all right," Eli says wearily. "But this isn't the place to talk about it."

Tori puts an arm around me. "It's okay."

But it's not okay. It might never be okay.

"Come on, Hector," Malik chides. "Get a grip."

You get a grip! I want to yell at him. *You didn't escape by the skin of your teeth like we did! You didn't see what we saw!*

Blinking back tears, I look at Eli and Tori, who heaved me up, dragged me along, and never once considered leaving me behind, even when my clumsiness slowed us down and threatened to get us caught. There's no way I could have made it without them.

Then I picture myself skimming across the duct and

resetting the grating in the nick of time. My shoulders straighten a little. There's also no way *they* could have made it without *me*.

My mother's words from long ago come back to me: I'm valuable.

I think of the conference room and wonder: Valuable *how?*

THINGS TO DO TODAY

- Piano Practice (1.5 hours)
- Ballet Practice (1 hour)
- Begin Diet (Goal weight: 99 lbs. Currently 101.5)
- Tread Water (18 minutes–preparation for big game)
- Work on Book with Tori
- Work on Serenity Day Project with Tori

I stare at the page for a few minutes and then cross out "Work on Book with Tori." *Your Own Backyard* has to be put on hold for the time being. Then I draw an arrow, moving our Serenity Day project to the top, and add the tag "prioritized."

Serenity Day will be here before we know it, but every time I mention our mural to Tori, she acts like it's something she vaguely remembers from a distant past. Never mind that it's 50 percent of our Contentment grade, and pretty much the most important thing we do in school all year.

It's more than just the project. When you've been best friends with somebody your whole life, you know when they're acting weird.

We're more like sisters than friends. I call her parents pseudo-Mom and pseudo-Dad, and she has her own drawer in my dresser so she'll have clothes available for spur-of-the-moment sleepovers. There are things in my closet that I don't remember if they're hers or mine. That's closer than close.

Until lately. Neither of us has slept at the other's house for weeks. We hardly even hang out these days. I can't quite explain it. Nothing's changed. We haven't had a big fight—it's nothing like that. It's just that she's never got time for me anymore. Even when we're together, it always seems like her mind is somewhere else.

What changed? Sure, I know I annoy some people—okay, Malik—because I'm kind of a perfectionist with my to-do lists. But Tori and I have been best friends since the cradle. If that stuff bugged her, it would have come out *years* ago.

What's so different about *now*?

My mom has a theory. "You girls are getting older, Amber. You're reaching the age where your interests might be, you know, evolving."

Translation: When you get to the upper grades, you start wanting to have boyfriends and girlfriends. I get that. How clueless does she think I am? You'd have to be locked in a closet not to notice that Tori has been brewing kind of a crush on Eli. But this is different. Something's bugging her. The last few days she's been pale, with dark circles under her eyes. I'm positive she's having trouble sleeping, although she insists she's fine.

When I finally nail her down to work on the project, I'm shocked by how little progress she's made. The background of the mural looks great—just the right hints of Carson National Forest, with the mountains in the distance. But she's barely started on the faces, which is annoying because last week she blew me off, saying she was too busy working on the faces!

I'm fuming in her attic studio, waiting for her to get out of the shower. How big a deal should I make out of this? I don't want to fight—that will only drive her away, and things are bad enough already. But if she gets a D, it's *my* D too. Even if I ace everything else in Contentment all year, the best I could hope for would be a C. And that just doesn't cut it when you're the teacher's kid.

Well, at least there's a set of pictures—head shots—on the table beside her easel in her attic studio. That means she *is* working on faces—or at least she's planning to. I leaf through them, curious to see who she's planning to use. It's a lot of kids, but plenty of adults too, especially people like Mom, Dr. Bruder, and Mr. Frieden, who are so prominent around town. There are a few Purple People Eater cards. She even has Bryan Delaney, who's the closest one to a real human being, since at least we know he has a real human wife. Our original idea was to substitute magazine faces for the Purples, who don't like to have their pictures taken. But that was before we knew about the cards.

Then I catch a glimpse of more photos. These aren't in the main stack; they're under the table in a small carton, half hidden under some tubes of oil paint. Did Tori forget these?

I fish them out and peer at the print on top. It isn't a head shot—it looks kind of like one of the bulletin boards at school. I squint at it. The heading says *Osiris 1: Eli Frieden*. It's dotted with pictures of Eli at all ages, including when he was a baby. There are other things too—papers and notes—but they're too small to read. A few seem to be on school stationery.

How serious has this crush become? Has Tori started an Eli collection? I frown. If that was true, she'd have a collection, not a picture of a collection!

I probe further. It's another bulletin board picture—this one's Hector Amani! I know for a fact, even without asking, that Tori doesn't have a crush on Hector!

And another one. It's *me*!

I hear Tori's footsteps on the attic stairs too late. "Okay, let's get to work—" She swallows the rest of it. Seeing what I'm looking at turns her to stone right there in the doorway.

"What *is* this?" I breathe.

I've known the girl since birth. I can honestly say I've never seen her so freaked out. "You can't tell anyone!" she begs. "Promise me, Amber!"

"Why do you have collages about people, with baby

pictures, and information? Why do you have one about *me*?"

She enters the room, still white-faced. "I can't tell you."

"You *have to* tell me!" I exclaim.

"You wouldn't understand," she says lamely.

"Try me!" I insist. "We're best friends! At least, we're supposed to be!"

"We are!" she cries. "Of course we are!"

"Then why can't you tell me what this is about?"

She fixes me with an intense stare. "Then promise you won't tell anyone! Not even your parents! I could get into *so* much trouble over this! You can't imagine how much!"

At this point, I'm pretty freaked out myself. It isn't just what Tori's saying, but the fact that she believes it a million percent. Whatever's going on here, something about it has her scared to death. "Okay. Take it easy. I promise."

She's silent a moment, then says, "This isn't going to be easy for you to hear, but the adults in this town have been—monitoring us."

"That's it?" I'm astounded. "That our parents keep an eye on us?"

"It's not what you think," she says emphatically. "They're studying us the way a scientist studies the stuff in test tubes and on slides. When Randy said something's screwy here—"

"*Randy?*" I explode. "Is that what this is all about? Randy is *Randy*! He's never taken anything seriously since the day he was born, and you've let him ruin Serenity for you! Don't you get it? We won the lottery, Tori! Only a handful of us get to grow up in the most wonderful, peaceful, amazing town there's ever been! But thanks to *Randy* and that stupid note, you can't even see it anymore!"

I want so much to reach her, but fear has made her completely close herself off.

"Remember," she persists, "you promised you wouldn't tell. Even if you think you're helping me, you're not."

What has her so scared? She's with *me*; her parents love her; our town looks after us 100 percent. How could she have found something wrong when everything's so totally right?

Suddenly, the answer is staring me right in the face via the images in my hand. Who else would have cradle-to-present-day photo records on a bunch of kids? This information could only belong to the school! Eli must have taken pictures of his father's files. Or they're Dr. Bruder's files, and Malik got ahold of them. Either way, it's private stuff that's been stolen, or at least spied on. Nobody lucky enough to grow up here should even *think* about doing that!

I know violence is bad, but I could smack Randy Hardaway. His note has become like a virus spreading among the kids in this town. If it can affect Tori, it can affect anybody.

"I don't even know you anymore, Tori. Can't you see this Randy thing is poisoning everyone? It's got people thinking so cockeyed that they don't even know what's right anymore! Life is perfect here, but how long will that last when there's anger, and lying, and secrets? What's next, huh? Murder?"

She's blank. "What's murder?"

I'm almost in tears. "Keep on like this and you'll find out soon enough! I don't want to do my Serenity Day project with you! I don't want to be your friend at all!"

I storm out of the studio and stomp downstairs. I'm tempted to march in and tell her parents how confused she is, but she swore me to secrecy. I promised, and in Serenity, we always keep our word.

16

ELI FRIEDEN

You can take me out of the Plastics Works, but you can't take the Plastics Works out of me.

That conference room is still with me. The whiteboards are burned onto my retinas so that I'm looking at them night and day regardless of whether my eyes are closed or open.

OSIRIS 1
ELI FRIEDEN

I'm not the only one still reeling from our mission to the factory. The simple process of describing it to Malik on the way home from the factory was almost as harrowing as living through it the first time. In a way, it was worse. What we found was so bizarre that it was almost like a movie plot. Telling it to another person made it real. And when we finally split up to go to our separate homes in that very early morning, we were in a daze. We discovered something momentous about ourselves, but what did it mean?

Even now that I've had time to think it over, I'm no closer to an answer. True, we learned a lot: the factory is a sham; the news and information we get is carefully screened and edited; the Purple People Eaters are spying on the town. Weirdest of all, eleven of us—but for some reason, not everybody—are being studied, and always have been.

I run my mind over the names. What's different about us? Why me and not Randy? Why Hector and not Stanley? Why Tori and not Melissa? *Special*—that was the word Randy used. Okay, I'm special, but what's so unspecial about him?

Two observations:

1) The "special eleven" have no siblings; we're only children.

2) All of us are between the ages of eleven and thirteen.

It doesn't say much. Three of the un-special group are

also only children, and nearly half of them fall into our age range. So my observations are probably worthless.

Every day after school, I meet with Malik, Tori, and Hector. We go over the pictures on my iPad in an attempt to understand what we saw in the conference room.

It's hard to make out all of what's on the whiteboards. We have to zoom in on one section at a time to blow up the writing. It's not a perfect system, because the words get fuzzier as they get bigger, so there's still a lot we can't read.

Bottom line: We knew we were being watched, but we had no idea of the extent of it. Our whiteboards contain accounts of temper tantrums we threw as toddlers, and details of how pleased or disappointed we were with Christmas and birthday presents we received when we were barely older than that. The monitoring is even more intense at school, where hidden surveillance cameras record everything we do, even the desserts we take on the "honor system" after lunch.

"Aw, come on!" exclaims Malik, the undisputed dessert-boosting champion. "There's no way I took five hundred and eighty-one cookies!"

"Cameras don't lie, Malik," grins Hector.

"You're not so perfect yourself, man," Malik retorts.

"Or should I say 'cheater.' That's what it says on *your* whiteboard."

"I didn't cheat," Hector contends. "I didn't stop *you* from cheating off *me*. It's a totally different thing."

"So what about this, huh? *'Failure to report grade inflation.'* That's all you, man."

"It's not my fault Mrs. Laska marked some of my tests wrong." Hector defends himself.

"Yeah," his best friend challenges, "but you didn't exactly break your neck to tell her your score was too high."

"If she's such a good teacher, she should be able to add."

"That's not it," Tori puts in thoughtfully. "Mrs. Laska must have known the grades were too high. Otherwise, how could she make a note that you didn't come forward to correct your score?"

"That's even stupider than counting people's cookies," Malik scoffs. "Why would a teacher give you the wrong grade *on purpose?*"

"They're testing us," I conclude. "Like when you get an extra-large horseshoe on Serenity Day, do you turn it in for a normal-sized one? They're trying to see how honest we are—or how honest we aren't," I add with a pointed look at Malik.

"It's just cookies!" Malik pleads. "It's not like I tried to rip off their precious Serenity Cup!"

"But just in case, they've got a camera on that too," Tori reminds us. "For all we know that's another test."

"But why should they *care*?" Hector wonders.

"When you think about it," I muse, "all these things are tests of character. Are we honest or not? How do we react to disappointment? Look at the stuff on water polo—it isn't who scores goals or wins games, who's a good player and who's so-so. It's all about who's aggressive, who uses the ball as a weapon, who's willing to do anything to win."

"Do all towns keep this kind of information on their kids?" Hector wonders.

"No way," Malik says stoutly. "Even here they don't keep tabs on everybody—just eleven of us. The Osiris people. That must be what makes us *special*."

"Osiris is the Egyptian god of the afterlife," I tell them. "Most of his stories are about dying or getting reborn or coming back from the underworld. I usually ask my dad or Mrs. Laska about this kind of stuff. I'm not asking this time."

We pore over every inch of the whiteboards, and it's

just more of the same: details upon details, our whole lives broken down into hundreds of mini-tests. The pictures of the conference table are even less helpful. Glare from the fluorescent lighting and the glass surface make the papers almost unreadable. The clearest thing we can pull from it is more of a word puzzle than a sentence. The document looks important, with photographs, and headings in bold. The pictures are nothing but blobs, and after over an hour of trying to read the headline, the best we can come up with is:

ARTH   OM W G EN

"Well, that explains everything," Malik says bitterly.

"Could it be a code?" Hector muses.

"I doubt it," I tell him. "Everything else is in plain English. We're just missing too many letters."

"There's no Osiris in there," Tori observes. "Or Serenity."

"It could be a person's name," Hector suggests. "Arthur Somebody."

"Or Martha," Tori adds.

"That first word could also be *earth*," Malik points out sarcastically. "That's why we're special. We're aliens.

Mystery solved. My dad wears those bow ties to communicate with the mother ship up there in orbit—"

"It's no joke, Malik," I cut him off. "We're talking about our lives here, and this could be a big part of it."

"Well, it would help if we knew what this paper was supposed to be," Malik returns. "Why didn't you bother to figure out what you were looking at instead of just snapping pictures of everything?"

Tori is patient. "We didn't have time. There was a Purple coming down the stairs."

I stare at the letters, expecting the blanks to fill in and reveal the truth about eleven special people.

Lying in bed that night, I'm still staring when my iPad runs out of power and goes dark.

After Tuesday night's three-hour ordeal, I'm not relishing the thought of sneaking out to the Plastics Works just to hook up to their Wi-Fi. I remember the time we were able to connect just outside the gate at the base of the Fellowship hill. I can't very well hang out there with my iPad—not without attracting attention from the Purples. But maybe there's another spot, just beyond plant property, where I can look like I'm studying, yet still piggyback the signal leaking through the factory walls.

I head over there Friday after school, tracing the perimeter fence, watching my tablet for a Wi-Fi indicator. When I see it, I retreat a few paces to a place where I can sit on the grass and lean against a tree. The signal's still there. Perfect. I've got my backpack with me, so I spread a few books around. If anybody sees me, they'll think I'm doing homework.

I start with the page on the Boston Tea Party just to make sure I've got the real web. Then I carefully type the letters in the Google search box.

ARTH   OM W G EN

There's nothing. Actually, there's quite a lot, but all the results are based on keyword "arthritis."

In other words, Google can't figure this out any better than we can.

Garbage in, garbage out.

Undaunted, I do a search for "Osiris." It churns up millions of hits, not just for the Egyptian god, but for a shoe company, a health club, a hotel, a rock band, and hundreds of other businesses with Osiris in their name. There's even a New York City delicatessen with a specialty sandwich called the Osiris—roast lamb on a pita topped with hummus in the shape of a pyramid. But when I add the parameter "Serenity, NM," the results go from all that to zero. Which means the worlds of Serenity and Osiris never intersect.

Except in that one conference room even Google doesn't know about.

Frustrated, I delete Osiris and search for Serenity on its own. That's when I make an astonishing discovery.

There is no such company as the Serenity Plastics Works.

How is that possible? I mean, the traffic cone thing is obviously a sham. But how can you overlook a giant building? What does Google think *that* is—a speed bump? Real or not, that factory is the center of the whole town!

I'm typing faster now, propelled by the liquid nitrogen pumping through my veins. There's also no Serenity Cable Company, no Serenity Channel One, no daily *Pax* newspaper.

I set down my iPad. I don't want to continue. I sense that something is coming at me like a runaway train. And whatever it is, I'm not going to have the strength to handle it. I'm tempted to sprint home and throw what I've just learned in my father's face, but of course, that's not an option.

What then? The answer is to push forward and try to find an explanation for this.

I rerun my Google search for "Osiris." There are so many hits—more than six million—I feel like I'm swimming in web links, struggling to stay afloat. There's no way I could ever go through all these sites in one lifetime. Not even with the others to help me.

There must be some way to narrow this down. I add other keywords: *Kids. Study.* There's no question that we're being studied. *Behavior.* That's part of it somehow. This pares the six million options down to a mere eighty thousand. To say I'm discouraged doesn't begin to describe it.

I'll never sift through it all, but I jump in, hoping something will catch my eye. Most of the links fall into two categories: study guides for kids learning about Egyptian mythology and podiatrists' studies on Osiris-brand shoes.

And then a word jumps out at me that has nothing to do with either mythology or shoes. It's instantly familiar, yet at first I have trouble placing it.

Hammerstrom.

That guy from the Purple People Eaters? Why would he come up? And then my heart begins to beat a little faster. A connection between Osiris and the Purples is a connection between Osiris and Serenity! This has to be important.

I click on the link, and a long document appears on my screen in a font that reminds me of an old-fashioned typewriter.

PROJECT OSIRIS

Project Osiris was a top secret experiment in human behavior proposed by
social scientist Dr. Felix Hammerstrom
and internet billionaire Tamara Dunleavy in the late 1990s . . .

Felix Hammerstrom? *Dr.* Felix Hammerstrom, the social scientist? My mind races back to the moment when the Surety took me off the chopper. *"Yes, Mr. Hammerstrom."* Those words weren't directed at the Purples; they were meant for my father! It was *Dad* who told me the name belonged to one of the rescue team. I believed him because, well, why would he lie?

Between then and now, though, he's lied at least twenty times. He's tried to wipe the truth out of my memory using brainwashing and pills. And now I'm staring at proof positive that he's one of the people behind this Project Osiris, whatever it is. I want to say I can't believe it, but I believe it all too easily.

My own father, and I didn't even know his real name!
I turn my attention back to the screen.

Osiris was designed to explore the concept of criminality from the perspective of nature versus nurture, i.e., is an individual born evil, or does he or she become evil through the influence of environment and experience? The results were expected to revolutionize our thinking with regard to the court and penal systems, and change crime and punishment as we know it.

The proposed experiment involved human cloning—the medical process of creating exact genetic twins of living people through the harvesting of their DNA. Under Osiris, clones would be created of the greatest criminal masterminds currently in prison. The babies born would be raised by surrogate parents in a fabricated community, geographically isolated and carefully protected from any exposure to illegality, violence, deception, and fraud. These subject children would be exact replicas of the very worst in human society, yet they would be free of all negative influence. Careful monitoring would reveal whether the clones have fulfilled the destiny of the evil in their DNA or if their decent and upright environment has nurtured gentle, law-abiding adults.

While initially hailed for its scientific approach to social issues, Project Osiris was criticized for its callous use of human life for research purposes and for its lack of endgame. The plan referred to a possible shift in experimental protocols once the cloned subjects reached fourteen years of age, but few details were provided on what would happen beyond then.

These concerns, along with the
international ban on human cloning, led
to the abandonment of Project Osiris
in 1999. Dr. Hammerstrom resigned
from the faculty of the University of
Colorado and dropped out of sight.
Tamara Dunleavy went into retirement
and now lives in seclusion on a ranch
outside Jackson Hole, Wyoming . . .

I'm as calm as I've ever been, but I know that's because I can't wrap my mind around what I've just seen. I'm tempted to dismiss it all as crazy, except that piece by piece, every element snaps into place like a jigsaw puzzle. Felix Hammerstrom—Felix Frieden. A fabricated, isolated community—Serenity. Streets with names like Fellowship, Harmony, Amity, Unity.

I read the article again and again until it's practically engraved on the inside of my skull casing. It's all true. It has to be. Every word of it.

Except for one thing: Project Osiris was never abandoned. Felix Hammerstrom changed his name and went ahead and did it in a place so far off the grid that no one would ever find out about it.

Project Osiris is *us*.

17

HECTOR AMANI

I understand now. It all makes sense to me.

Way back when I was a toddler in the sandbox—when I had that near miss with the rattlesnake—I finally understand my mother's words to my father.

You know how valuable he is.

It wasn't a mother's unconditional love for her baby. I'm not her baby. I'm nobody's baby. I'm not even human.

Well, technically, clones still count as human. Our bodies have the same vital organs, blood, tissue, and bone as real people. We eat, drink, sleep, and go to the bathroom just like everybody else.

No, when she said *valuable*, she meant exactly that. There are only ten others like me in the entire world—not just human clones, but clones of criminal masterminds.

That might be the hardest part of all to accept. I'm pretty smart and get good grades, but I don't feel like a mastermind. It makes me think of some kind of warped evil-genius type, trying to take control of the world. Come to think of it, I wouldn't mind being a little more in control—not of the whole world; just my little part of it. Especially where Mom and Dad are concerned. And maybe Malik.

Now, *Malik* I can see as a mastermind.

It's a pretty crazy thing for anybody to learn about himself. And craziest of all is what we still don't know: Yes, we're cloned from criminal masterminds, but which ones? Who are these arch-lawbreakers who are our exact genetic matches?

We're all shocked when Eli gives us the news that we're clones, but I'm slightly less shocked than the others. I've always sensed that I'm a little bit less than a person—not quite good enough, or brave enough, or handsome enough to make the cut. I never suspected I was created in a lab like space-age plastic or a revolutionary new zit cream. But those are just details.

Eli takes us out by the factory so we can read the article for ourselves. The story is a lot less science fiction than I expect. We all started out as cells in test tubes, but everything was kind of normal after that. We were placed inside host mothers for nine months and then we were born in the regular way. Our Serenity "parents"—the moms and dads we grew up with—are scientists working on Project Osiris. The nonspecial kids in town aren't clones like us; they're the natural children of other people attached to the experiment.

"I should have known," Tori whispers. "When I was working on the mural it was so obvious. There were family resemblances for some of the kids, but not us."

Considering the huge asteroid strike we've all experienced, our reaction is pretty quiet. There are a few tears, but mostly, we're too dazed to cry. There's so much to swallow: Our parents aren't our parents; we don't have parents; our entire lives are an experiment. Eli's had the most time to get used to it, but he's also the most devastated of the four of us. His "father" is the head of the whole thing—him and that billionaire lady, who doesn't seem to be part of it anymore.

"Who says we don't have family resemblances?" Malik mumbles. "Just not to our so-called parents. I wonder who I look like. Adolf Hitler, probably."

Eli shakes his head. "We can't be cloned from famous

criminals from a long time back. The people we come from are still alive—at least they were when we were"—his mouth twists—"made."

Tori covers her face with her hands. "I can't believe we're *criminals*. I can only imagine the terrible things we must have done!"

"Stop right there," Eli orders. "*We* haven't done anything. Even if we're exact doubles of people who've committed crimes, we're innocent. Don't ever forget that."

"That was the whole purpose of the experiment," I put in. "To prove that we can be good even though we're clones of bad people."

"That makes me feel so much better," Malik says sarcastically. "I'm a freak but I can be a *good* freak."

"We're only four of eleven clones," Tori moans. "How do we tell the others?"

It's a point. There are seven other Osiris clones in town who have no idea who they are. "Do we tell the others at all?" I amend Tori's question.

"No way," Malik says quickly.

"They're the same as us," Eli reasons. "They have a right to know."

Malik is adamant. "Half of them will think we're crazy

and the other half will freak out and blab."

"At least I have to tell Amber," Tori reasons. "She's my best friend."

"She's the *last* person you can tell," Malik argues. "She thinks Happy Valley is Shangri-la-dee-da. She'd never accept that the perfect life is really a sick experiment, courtesy of our loving families. She'll go straight to her parents to be reassured that God's in his heaven and all's right with the world. And then Project Osiris will know *we* know, which might ruin their research. You'll notice that web page doesn't mention what happens to us if we get contaminated by too much information."

I don't like the sound of that. "Malik—" It never occurred to me that our parents might try to harm us, but maybe that's because I've grown up *here*. In the real world, people harm each other every day. After all, what's the purpose of the Purple People Eaters? Not to protect a factory that isn't a factory, or to keep order in a town that's already 100 percent orderly. "You don't think that"—I shudder— "because we were *made* we can be, you know, *unmade*?"

"You mean killed?" Malik says bitterly. "Can't happen. Ever notice there's no cemetery in Happy Valley? Come to think of it, what have we been doing with dead people since 1937—eating them?"

"Stop it," Tori pleads. "There was never any 1937 for Serenity. They built it for *us*. And when Osiris is over, Serenity will probably disappear."

"Osiris is already over," Eli amends. "Once you know you're in an experiment, it's not an experiment anymore."

"Great," Malik comments. "The whole purpose behind our lives just expired." He has a knack for cutting right to the heart of the matter.

Eli shakes his head. "*Their* purpose for us might be gone. But our whole lives are still ahead of us. I don't know about you guys, but I intend to *live* mine."

"Good luck selling dear old Dad on that one," Malik drawls.

I've never been the happiest kid in town, and the fact that my parents are really scientists explains some of it, but not all. The Bruders, the Pritels, the Laskas—they're researchers too, the same as my folks. Yet they've been "parents" in a way mine have never been. Even an experiment needs to be loved. "We'll leave," I say suddenly.

"Yeah, right," snorts Malik.

"Seriously," I insist. "You're always talking about leaving Serenity because it's so boring. Well, that's exactly what we'll be doing. We'll just be doing it sooner."

They stare at me—Malik in uncertainty, Tori in

amazement. It takes me a moment to decipher Eli's expression. It's something I'm not used to: respect. For the first time in my life, I'm leading, not following.

"Hector's right," he says. "We're never going to be free of Osiris until we get out of this place."

"But we're just kids," Tori protests. "We're in the middle of nowhere. And there are only four of us, compared with close to two hundred who are going to try to stop us."

"It won't be easy," Eli concedes, "but if we got into the factory, we can do this too. With careful planning, it can be done."

"It's nothing like the factory!" Tori exclaims, her voice cracking a little. "That was three hours; this is *forever*! Maybe they aren't my parents in the usual way—but they're still my parents. Even if they lied to me—that doesn't mean I never want to see them again."

Malik studies his sneakers. He's hoping nobody notices, but the sun catches his eyes and they're moist. He's always complaining about how his mom babies him, and how embarrassed he is by his dad. Still, the idea of leaving them has him pretty shaken up.

Aloud, he says, "Count me in. If Hector's got the guts, so do I."

I'm floored. Malik is the strong one, and here he is, looking to me for courage.

I realize that I have less to lose than he does. I have a comfortable life with two researchers acting as my mother and father. He has a *family*.

"I can't leave my parents," Tori barely whispers.

"We don't have parents," Malik informs her. "We have zookeepers."

It hurts to hear it, even for me. My mom and dad should be the easiest of all to walk away from. But it doesn't work that way.

They're not our real parents, but they're the only ones we've ever known.

18

ELI FRIEDEN

Our home is filled with pictures of my poor dead mother. Dad's always lecturing me on what "Mom" would have wanted, and I have to live up to her high expectations. Not only is she ever present, but she's ever disappointed. Add to that my guilt that I can't conjure up a single memory of her—not a voice, not a touch, nothing.

Now I know why. She never existed.

I spend twenty minutes with a magnifying glass and their wedding picture. Apparently, I'm not the only one in the house who knows how to use Photoshop.

I shouldn't be so amazed. Anyone twisted enough to create Project Osiris could certainly come up with a loving wife and mother. It should be easy compared with cloning eleven children from the DNA of maximum-security prisoners, and inventing a whole town and way of life to raise them in.

My father isn't a mayor and a principal, he's a scientist—a *mad* scientist. And he isn't even my father. What he really is, I now realize, is the world's greatest liar—his name, his wife, his town, his plastics factory, his newspaper, our so-called education, where one fact in ten might be true. The longer I think about it, the more lies I see, swirling around me like a fog.

Example: since we have no real parents, all our last names have to be made up, right? I spent a couple of hours on Google Translate last night, and I learned that our surnames mean things like friendship, brother, peace, and love in different languages. Even *Pax* is just the Latin word for peace. Like our street signs and our water polo teams and the name of the town itself, it's all part of the Osiris experiment: Can exact copies of criminal masterminds turn out to be decent citizens if you call their street Harmony instead of Oak?

It's an interesting question, if you're not the poor dummy who's been created purely to be a lab subject. That's not a fun thing to carry around either—the knowledge that you're an exact replica of a horrible criminal. Malik was just joking about Adolf Hitler, but we could easily be cloned from someone who's robbed other people or even killed them. Even though I haven't done anything wrong, every chromosome in the DNA of that guy who did such terrible things—every brain cell that made the choice to act that way—I've got that too.

It's scary and infuriating—and the anger is the scariest part. Was it anger that turned my DNA twin into a criminal mastermind? Does that mean I'm already on my way? And how do I stop it? *Can* it be stopped? Everything I do—is it me deciding, or is it him?

Malik has also been thinking about where his genes came from, but he doesn't seem to be as bothered by it. He refers to his DNA donor as "my guy," as in, "I can't wait to blow this Popsicle stand so I can go find my guy."

"He's not your uncle, you know," Hector reminds him. "He's more like an older evil twin."

"I'll bet he's in NYC," Malik daydreams. "Convenient—I was planning to head that way myself."

"The reason they got his DNA is because he was in *jail*," I point out. "Chances are, he's still there. Master criminals get long sentences."

"The jail hasn't been built that can hold my guy. He must be a real player. Please don't let me get the bonehead who got arrested for jaywalking."

Like this is a contest to see who's cloned from the coolest felon.

"I don't want to meet mine." It's one of the rare times Hector doesn't agree with Malik.

"Aw, come on," Malik shoots back. "Your guy is a cinch to find. Just scour the prison system for somebody four foot six doing time for felony pain-in-the-butt."

Hector doesn't take the bait. "I don't care about that stuff," he says seriously. "I just want to get out of here and make a fresh start."

"So what are we waiting for?" Malik turns back to me. "When do we make our move?"

"Tori still hasn't decided if she's coming with us," I tell him.

"Forget her, man!" Malik exclaims. "I've got nothing against Tori, but we can't just chill forever while she makes up her mind."

I dig in my heels. "We need her. Remember the factory? We never could have pulled it off without her. We've got to get this right, Malik. If we're caught, there won't be any second chances, even if our parents have to chain us up in our rooms."

"Well, tell her to hurry up," Malik says irritably. "If we wait too long, she'll break down and blab everything to

Mommy and Daddy."

To me, that's even more reason not to push her. Too much pressure might make her snap in the wrong direction and come clean to her parents.

Hey, I totally get her reluctance to turn her life upside down. It goes far beyond working up the courage to break away from her family. Escaping this place is going to be *hard*. The next town is eighty miles away, and we have no transportation other than bikes. There are four of us against close to two hundred Osiris types and Purple People Eaters, and they have cars and a helicopter. And even if we do get away, what then? We're underage, we don't know anybody outside Serenity, and we have no idea how things work in the world. Our education may or may not bear any resemblance to reality, and even the books we've read and the movies we've seen might have been edited by Osiris scientists.

One idea is to go to the Taos police and tell them who we are, and what's been done to us. Maybe they'll shut down Project Osiris and rescue the other seven who are like us. But that's if they believe us in the first place—it's a pretty crazy story coming from a bunch of kids. What evidence do we have? A few dozen pictures of the conference room? They're barely readable on my iPad—a whole lot of "*ARTH   OM W G EN*," but very little that's concrete. The real stuff on the whiteboards can easily be taken down and hidden. It'll end up our word against our parents'.

For all we can predict, we'll be in trouble for the crimes our DNA twins committed, or simply for being clones in the first place. What if that's illegal?

If we do manage to get away, we'll have to take things as they come, and make decisions on the fly. The prospect of it freaks me out—just not enough to stay here and live my life the Osiris way.

So for the moment, we're biding our time, making mental plans, and trying to act as if nothing is up. I smile through the lump in my throat, and remind myself that the guy across the breakfast table is not my father, but a scientist named Felix Hammerstrom. I am quiet and obedient, the perfect son. I slave over a Serenity Day project that with all my heart I hope not to be here to present. I write endless details of President Roosevelt's 1937 visit, an event that never happened, regardless of what it says on our fake internet. I fill Excel spreadsheets with manufacturing statistics about our fake plastics factory. I quote fake articles from the *Pax* about how our town is tops in the state, the country, the hemisphere, the world, the solar system, the Milky Way.

In school, I keep my grades up and my mouth shut. If Mrs. Laska finds out what I've been thinking about in Meditation, she'll definitely dock my Contentment score.

In gym, I'm a beast in the pool. The emotions I'm suppressing in every other part of my life are coming through in water polo. Luckily, I've got an excuse. I tell Mrs. Delaney I'm striving to make myself a counterbalance to Malik's overpowering physical play.

"It's fine to be aggressive," she tells me. "But you're swimming like you're trying to hurt the water. You move better with the relaxed, measured stroke you always use."

"I'll try harder next time."

The words come out so automatically that she can tell it's lip service.

She's quiet a moment, chewing this over. Then: "Remember what I said when I came to your house that time? That if you ever need someone to talk to, you can count on me?"

I do remember, and the truth is I like talking to Mrs. Delaney. I always sensed she was different from the other adults in town, and now I have proof. She must have been just a kid in the early days of Project Osiris. Does she know the whole truth about what's going on here? It's impossible to tell, but I hope not. I want to believe she's the kind of person who'd never go along with the Serenity scam.

I realize something unexpected: When I'm gone from this nightmare town, I might feel sad about leaving my dad, mostly out of habit and brainwashing. But she's the only one I'll actually *miss*. "You're awesome, Mrs. Delaney. I'll never forget you."

She looks puzzled. "Forget me? I'm not going anywhere. I just got here." Her playful grin disappears as her eyes narrow. "Are *you*—going somewhere?"

My heart leaps up into my throat and I very nearly choke on it. How could I have said something so stupid? "Of course not," I manage to rasp. "I never go anywhere."

She studies me for what seems like a long time. At last, she says, "Sorry, I must have misunderstood. Now go and change. Maybe try a swim at home tonight. Take it nice and easy—get your regular stroke back."

As soon as the locker room door shuts behind me, I slide down the wall to the floor and sit there, hyperventilating. After worrying so much about Tori, I almost gave it all away in a nothing conversation about water polo.

It begins to sink in that the longer we delay, the greater the likelihood that one of us will slip up and spill the beans. And then we can kiss any chance at freedom good-bye.

19

TORI PRITEL

Mom makes my favorite dinner tonight (mac and cheese with spicy bread crumb topping) and doesn't give me a hard time until I start my fourth helping.

It's love. It has to be. Nothing has changed. A few whiteboards and an old article on the internet can't wipe out a family.

Steve looks up from the depths of my homework. "They're simple equations, Torific. We went over this last week. *And* the week before."

"I'm an artist, Steve," I tell him. "I obviously don't *do* math."

"As long as it's part of the curriculum," Mom says, "you obviously do."

I know they're not my biological parents, but I refuse

to believe I'm just an experiment to them. I mean every bit as much to them as a real daughter would.

How can I leave them?

On the other hand, I saw the conference room of the plastics factory, and I saw the *Pax* office where our bogus reality is crafted for our eyes only. I read the description of Project Osiris that could only be us—raised up to our ears in harmony and contentment in a hermetically sealed town. This can't be a misunderstanding; there's no way we got it wrong somehow. It's awful, but it's the (awful) truth.

Every time my parents had to work late (a vital shipment of traffic cones urgently needed somewhere!), that was a bald-faced lie. They were probably in that conference room reporting on me, making notes for my whiteboard. Worse, even before I was born, when Project Osiris was supposed to be canceled because it was immoral, my parents signed on anyway to raise the clone of some criminal mastermind (me).

Maybe they did it for the money. Serenity's a pretty rich place. They had student loans to pay off. What choice did they have?

I want to believe that *so* much! But it still doesn't explain everything.

So how can I stay?

Maybe it's this: We artists are hopeless romantics, and there's this romantic vision that I just can't shake: infant Tori placed into the arms of the two researchers; it's love at first sight!

It could have happened that way. It *probably* happened that way.

But is that enough?

I'm getting a lot of pressure from Malik and Hector to make up my mind once and for all. Eli's being a lot cooler, but deep down, he's more torn up than any of us. After all, Mr. Frieden is the head of Project Osiris.

Whoops. Not Mr. Frieden; Dr. Hammerstrom.

To make life even more difficult, Amber has gone from best friend to ex–best friend, and barely even talks to me. This is pretty awful because we're still supposed to be doing our Serenity Day project together. So there she is, in *my* studio, painting the background of *my* mural.

They say silence can be deafening. Well, this is the opposite of that. Our silence is just silent. We might as well be in deep space.

We're closer than sisters, and I know something that

explains *everything* about her life and her world. And what do I tell her? Nothing.

Some friend *I* am.

It's beyond weird—or maybe not. Maybe the criminals we're cloned from are the strong, silent type.

My climbing wild roses have stopped climbing halfway up the trellis, looking like they could make it to the top if only someone would pay attention to them. That someone being me.

Along with everything else I've been neglecting, like my Serenity Day project and my best friend, I've been neglecting my plants too.

Steve says you can't grow roses in the desert, and it's turned into one of our classic *no-you-can't, yes-I-can* things. So I'm determined to grow them, paint a picture of them, and present him with the finished product, nicely framed, on his next birthday.

I scale the trellis with a handful of twist ties so I can train the tendrils to reach for the sky. The feeling of being off the ground against the stucco is eerily familiar—I can almost see myself clinging to the wall of the Plastics Works after the rope came loose. It was very nearly a real disaster. I'm lucky the factory had so many niches and handholds that let me scramble to the top.

Or maybe it wasn't luck. I look at our wall and see just as many spots to hang on to. If I can climb a factory in the pitch-black, a regular house should be a breeze. Intrigued, I work my way past the roses, past the trellis, and up toward the second story. I can't explain it, but it just seems *obvious* to me—like the handholds and footholds have been outlined in Magic Marker. I'm pretty high up, but I'm not afraid at all. My sneakers are established in the mortar course between adobe bricks, and my hands have a firm grip on the sill beneath my parents' bedroom window.

I hear their voices from inside, and stifle an impulse to raise myself up and knock on the sash. They'd probably have a fit. I'm about to start down when a word from my mother reaches me, and it stops me cold: "Osiris 3."

Osiris 3—that's Malik!

I hang there, waiting for more.

"I don't like it," I hear my father say. "The kid's not just a number. You're talking about one of Tori's best friends."

"It's always been in the protocols." This from Mom again. "The older ones will be fourteen soon. Any toxic element has to be weeded out for the good of the group."

"This isn't what I signed up for." Steve sounds stressed. "When does he go?"

"We don't want to spoil Serenity Day," Mom replies. "After that, he's out."

One of my feet comes loose, and I lurch, momentarily swinging from the sill. All at once, this climb isn't so much fun, and growing roses in the desert seems like a pointless waste of time.

I ease myself down the wall, scratching my legs on the thorns. It probably stings, but I don't even notice. A few overheard words can hurt so much more.

We already know about our parents, but this is the first time one of us has heard it straight from their mouths.

Any toxic element has to be weeded out. First Malik. Who's next?

Most important of all, what exactly does *weeded out* mean?

I suddenly realize that I'll never know, because we can't risk sticking around long enough to see it happen.

I head for the Frieden house. I feel like I'm going to throw up on the way over there, yet now that the decision is made, I won't go back on it. Funny, I never considered myself a strong-willed person, but I suddenly understand that I must be cloned from one.

Eli opens the door. He looks nervous when he sees it's me.

I swallow hard. "I've made up my mind."

Malik tries to play it cool when I tell him about my parents' conversation. We can tell he's freaked out, though, because he's breathing a little too hard, like he's just come from water polo practice.

"Toxic element, huh?" His usual bored drawl doesn't quite come off. "So what else is new?"

"The Pritels don't understand you like we do!" Hector tries to cheer him up. "The things you say—*we* get that you don't always mean them!"

Malik turns angry. "You think this is only the Pritels? They're just who we heard it from. This is *everybody*— all the adults—" Suddenly, he's deathly quiet. "My own parents. They want this too. They think I should be— *weeded*."

"We have no way of knowing what 'weeded' means," I remind him.

He's bitter. "I doubt your folks were talking about gardening."

"It doesn't matter what it means," Eli jumps in. "We

won't be here to find out. Now, let's work on our plan."

What we come up with is pretty simple. (It has to be, since we know nothing beyond our own borders.) We sneak out after everyone else has gone to sleep, jump on our bikes, and meet at the edge of town on Old County Six just beyond the surveillance cameras.

We're obviously flying by the seat of our pants, hoping that what little information we have is right. Based on a map Eli saw on the factory's internet, we think there's a rail line passing not far to the south of us. The trouble is the rail map had no Serenity on it. So our starting point is just an educated guess, based on the location of Taos and Carson National Forest. We could be just a few miles from the tracks; we could be fifty or sixty.

"It's not a big difference on a map," Malik observes, "but I bet it's pretty noticeable when you're pedaling."

The planning meeting is pretty tense, and not just because we're short on details. We're scared to death, and even more scared of what might happen if we stay. Malik is obviously the one in immediate crisis, but we'll all turn fourteen eventually. Eli's birthday comes even a few days before Malik's. We're all in danger of being weeded, whatever that is.

"Can I ask a practical question?" puts in Hector.

"What do we do when the train comes?"

"Simple," Malik replies. "We throw you onto the tracks, and while they're picking up the pieces with a shrimp fork, the rest of us sneak aboard."

"Be serious, Malik," I scold.

"Who's joking? I'm the toxic element, remember?"

"No more than the rest of us," Hector soothes. "We're cloned from the toxic hall of fame."

"Then I guess I win," Malik says with a mixture of acid and pride. "Rah, rah. It's not easy to be worst when you're raised with the scum of the earth."

Eli steers the conversation back to the plan. "We won't know how to handle the train until we're there and it's actually happening. I'm hoping for a really slow, heavy freight where we can climb onto a flat car. But we'll just have to wait and see."

"As long as we're away from here," intones Malik, his expression haunted.

"I wish I could see my parents' reaction," says Hector with a mixture of relish and dread, "when they wake up and realize their guinea pig is gone."

That gives me a jolt. "I was kind of thinking of leaving my parents a note—you know, to tell them I still love them in spite of everything."

Eli practically jumps down my throat. "No way! What if they wake up in the middle of the night and see it? They'll be on the phone with the Purples in a heartbeat."

My eyes fill with tears. "I just can't stand the thought that this is forever. Maybe someday—I mean, a long time from now—down the line—we can, you know, visit . . ." My voice trails off.

"Yeah, sign me up for that," Malik drawls. "I can't wait to come back so they can weed me."

The date is set: tomorrow night. With the clock ticking down on Malik, we have to act fast.

Also, if we delay too long, someone is bound to chicken out. (I'm sure the guys think it'll be me.)

I sleepwalk through school the next day, retreating into my own thoughts because it's the only way to keep from losing it. I register everything as "my last"—my last taste of Mom's scrambled eggs; my last water polo practice; my last Meditation class; my last meal at the kitchen table in our house.

Steve picks up on something. "Is everything okay, Torific? You seem kind of distracted."

"I was just thinking about art school at the Sorbonne," I tell him. "Paris has the Louvre, the Musée d'Orsay, and a lot of other great museums."

It's a surefire way to get him off the topic of why I'm acting weird. Tomorrow, I know, an entire guided tour of the Louvre will be uploaded to my computer—anything to keep me from wanting to go there.

Poor Steve. He has no idea that I'm already on my way.

There's just one thing left undone, and I have to take care of it. After dinner, I climb the stairs to my studio. There, stretched out on the big table, is the Serenity Day mural. Our project—Amber's and mine. It's finished. Not my best work, but I have to admit it looks pretty decent, maybe because it depicts a way of life that I'm never going to have again.

I roll it up and take it over to Amber's house—a walk I've made a million times, although not lately and not feeling the way I do now.

It's a good thing Mr. and Mrs. Laska are home, or Amber probably wouldn't let me in. I'm grateful to her, though. She's kept her promise. She never told anyone about the pictures of the whiteboards. All she did was stop talking to me, which was painful enough.

Eventually we're up in her room, and I unroll our mural. "What do you think?"

"Good," she says without even looking at it. "Why did you bring it here?"

"So you can take it to Serenity Day."

"Why can't *you* take it to Serenity Day?"

This is obviously a question I have no answer for. So I just remind her, "It's your project too."

She rolls it up again, looking exasperated and a little sad. "Fine. I'll bring it in."

"It was fun working on it together," I blurt.

"Right. Fun."

I'm floundering now. After being so close that our lives were practically merged together, it's beyond terrible to leave things like this. "I'm sorry we've been fighting. If you think about it, we've been friends a lot longer than we've been, you know, not."

She's not answering anymore. She just wants me to go. And anyway, there's no point in rambling on, because the one thing I really want to say is also the one thing I can't:

Good-bye.

20
AMBER LASKA

THINGS TO DO TODAY
- ?????

I concentrate on the paper, but for some reason, I can't come up with a single item to put on it. All I can think of is Tori.

What's up with her? I mean besides the fact that she's turned on Serenity because of a note from *Randy.*

She's my best friend and all we do is fight. I'm so upset. I don't have *time* to be upset. I'm a busy person!

This is stupid. I get things done by making lists and budgeting my time. Staring at a blank page doesn't fit into my lifestyle.

- Ballet Practice (1.5 hours)
- Piano Practice (1 hour) . . .

It's not rocket science. These are on the list every day. What else?

A flicker of blue catches my eye. It's the corner of the rolled-up mural leaning against my desk. The sky—*my* sky. I'm the one who colored it in, even if I didn't contribute much else from an artistic standpoint.

You're doing it again, I check myself. *Concentrate on the list . . .*

But it bugs me: Why would she bring the project over to my house when it can just as easily sit in her studio? In my room, it's more likely to get stepped on or tripped over.

Obviously, it was just an excuse to talk to me. But what did she really say?

"I'm sorry we've been fighting . . . We've been friends a lot longer than we've been, you know, not."

Okay, she wants to make up and be friends again. I want that too. But there's no way I'm going to stand by and listen to her conspiracy theories.

Get back to the list . . .

But what if she isn't trying to make up? If you look at it

another way, her words sound almost like something you'd say to a person you're never going to see again. What if she brought the mural to me because she won't be around to hand it in herself?

My heart begins to race. Could that be what this means? That Tori is planning to run away from home?

Impossible! Who would do something so drastic? Where could she go, and how would she get there?

I sit down on the edge of my bed, my heart racing. This is a crazy thing to do! There's no way she can make it alone. A thought hits me. Could she have others going with her? Eli, maybe? Randy's note was meant for him. Or Malik, who never shuts up for a second about his intention to "blow this Popsicle stand"?

In the end, it doesn't matter. I tell myself, even if they do get away, so what? They'll be kids, living by their wits in some filthy city. The idea of Tori, surrounded by crime and violence like I read about in that *USA Today*, makes my stomach clench.

I can't let Tori make a mistake like this. We were best friends once, even if we aren't anymore. On the other hand, she made me promise not to tell anyone what I saw in her studio. I can't go back on my word.

I take a deep breath and picture a reinvented list:

- Catch Tori in the act.
- Convince her not to do this.

Even if she's turned on Serenity, surely I can make her see that dying in the desert is a worse option.

Catch her in the act: We live at the end of Harmony Street, and my bedroom window has a perfect view of her front door. I'll just have to keep watch until she makes her move.

Serenity Day is less than a week away.

Whatever's going to happen will happen soon.

Midnight comes and goes, and there's less than nothing going on.

At first, I read *Little Women* while watching out the window, but my desk lamp casts too much glare onto the glass. I'm bored, tired, and starting to feel dumb. It won't look good if the teacher's daughter falls asleep in class tomorrow. I stay alert by reminding myself that doing the right thing is the Third Rule of Contentment, after 1) being satisfied with what you have and 2) being honest in all ways.

My head snaps up suddenly, and I realize that I must have fallen asleep. Not acceptable. I might only have one chance to stop Tori. No way am I going to miss it. When I feel myself nodding off again, I dig my fingernails into my wrist until it hurts.

I'm still squeezing when the door of the Pritel house opens and Tori slips out onto the porch, a backpack over her shoulder.

I've already got sneakers on for a quick and quiet exit. There's a moment of panic when I lose her. She was right outside her door just a few seconds ago! How could she disappear so quickly?

And then she flashes into view, passing through the glow of a streetlight. She's farther away than I thought she'd be, and I see why. She's on her *bike*! That's something I never considered—you can't think of everything, even with a to-do list. I race back to the garage and grab my Schwinn, wincing at each bang and bump that puts me in danger of waking Mom and Dad. By the time I maneuver it out the small door—I can't use the automatic one, which shakes the whole house—Tori is completely gone from sight. No, there she is, under another light on Old County Six, at least a half a mile ahead. There are two—no, three—other riders with her. They're heading east out of town.

I pedal off, desperate to catch up, but they're pedaling

hard too. By the time I reach Old County Six, I'm a little closer, but not much. There are no streetlights outside of town, so I'm having trouble keeping them in view. Luckily, the night sky is usually clear over Serenity and the stars hang like grapes, close and brilliant. A half-moon contributes to the general glow.

I turn on the jets. I've got to reach them before we're so far that by the time I can convince them to turn back, someone will notice we're missing.

I go all out. The lights of Serenity fall away behind me and I'm under the canopy of the heavens, too, which makes it easier to keep my quarry in sight. I'm within a quarter mile now, and gaining. They're riding slow and steady, pacing themselves for a long journey, but I'm on a wind sprint. After Tori, I identify Malik first, a big hulking figure. And the smaller silhouette—Hector! Where Malik is, can he be far behind? As for the tall, lean one—

At that moment, Eli turns around, almost as if he can sense my thoughts. Even in the low light, I see his eyes bulge at the sight of someone following them. He says something to the others, and the four of them start pedaling like mad. They're pulling away again, and it's taken most of my strength to get this close. I haven't got another burst of energy in me.

I make a split-second decision. "*Tori!*" I bellow.

She slows down, falling behind the others, but not stopping. "Amber?" she calls in disbelief. "What are you doing here?"

My breath is coming out in gasps. I blow all the energy I've got left to pull up to her. "Please stop—"

She bikes on, but I can tell she's pretty shaken. "We're not stopping. Come with us if you want, but we're not turning back."

"But—this is—crazy—" I'm panting now; I can't seem to get any words out. How am I going to convince them if I can't even talk? But if I pause to catch my breath, I'll fall behind again. . . .

I keep riding. If I let them go, I'll never get the chance to influence them. Yet every second is taking us farther from Serenity. The glimmer of town is long gone.

The fatigue is getting to me. It's worse than the end of a water polo match, because I've got a headache, and I'm starting to feel sick to my stomach. I know I'm still a couple of pounds off my goal weight, but how am I so out of shape?

There's a commotion up ahead. I look away from Tori in time to see Hector topple off his bike onto the soft shoulder. I squint through the blinding pressure behind my eyes as Malik jumps off and makes for his fallen friend. Before he can get there, he doubles over in sudden distress and throws up. Beside me, Tori does the same. Her bicycle hits the pavement, and she sits down in the middle of the highway, gagging. I retch, barely managing to hold on to my own dinner. My head is pounding so hard that I'm having trouble focusing on where I am and why I'm straddling a bike. What's going on?

Eli staggers toward us, holding the top of his head like it's about to fly off. "Get out of the road!" he rasps, white-faced. "Hide the bikes!"

"Why?" I groan. It's obvious that something horrible is happening to all of us at the same time, but how will *hiding* help?

"I've had this before!" Eli croaks, dragging my Schwinn off the pavement into high brush. "It'll be here soon!"

"*What*'ll be here soon?" Tori breathes.

That's when we notice it, faint, but unmistakable in the silent night—the distant rotor blades of a helicopter.

Malik hears it, too, and his alarm gives him the strength to lift his head up. "Purples!"

"We'll never outrun a chopper!" Hector moans.

Eli spins around, frantically scanning the darkness.

"There!" He points to an oddly shaped rock formation with a generous overhang. "Get under that!"

"Why?" I demand. "They're coming to help us!"

"They're coming to arrest us!" Malik counters.

"But they're on our side!" I plead.

"Think!" Eli commands. "How do you feel? The headache; the sick stomach—we all have it. There must be some kind of invisible barrier around town, and we just hit it!"

I obey, not because I agree, but because my splitting head makes it impossible to think straight. I feel rather than see myself bumbling through the brush along with the others, heading for the shelter of that rock. If we weren't so debilitated and in such pain, we'd make great comedy, teetering along on unsteady legs like baby giraffes learning how to walk.

"The bikes too!" Eli chokes. "Take the bikes!"

The effort to turn around and go back for his bicycle drops Hector to the ground again. In a Herculean feat of strength, Malik ends up dragging two bikes plus Hector. Eli tries to help Tori and me, but nobody is much help to anybody. We're just too sick. I finally give in and throw up too. I taste acid in my throat.

We can see the lights of the chopper now, and the roar

of the engine is growing louder. A cone-shaped search beam sweeps over the ground. Weakened as we are, it spurs us into action. Wildly, we cram ourselves and our gear under the overhang, and hunker there, trembling with fear and discomfort. For a long, terrifying moment, the light flickers all around us.

Malik has a death grip on my arm, and I whimper, "Let me signal them!"

Tori sounds exhausted. "For God's sake, Amber, haven't you figured it out yet? Serenity is a prison and we just climbed over the wall!"

"It's not true!" I blubber. "It can't be true!" But the evidence is right in front of me. It's rocking all of us, like it rocked Eli before. I struggle to focus my reeling mind on one point in Eli's story. "Okay, if it's happening to everybody, and it's happening to Eli again, why didn't it happen to Randy?"

"Because Randy wasn't one of the prisoners," Eli shoots back. "And we are. Even you, Amber."

Crouched beside me, Malik utters a single moan, and passes out, his head lolling onto Hector. My arm is free. I can run out into the beacon and get us all rescued.

I hesitate. Even though they're not making sense, I have no better explanation for our current state. Tori and

Eli talked about two main ideas in Randy's note: First, some of us are special, but not Randy; and second, that's why Eli got sick and Randy didn't.

As we huddle in agony beneath the overhang, the note doesn't seem like such a joke anymore. I can't accept everything they're telling me—especially not with my brain on fire. But it's enough to prevent me from running out and waving down the chopper.

A moment later, the searchlight is gone, and the road is dark again. The engine noise diminishes as the craft moves away.

"They're giving up?" Hector asks through gritted teeth.

Eli shakes his head, wincing at the motion. "Probably just continuing the search. The invisible barrier must be a circle around the whole town."

"What are we going to do?" Hector rasps.

Malik is awake again. "I'm not going back. I say we push on. If this is a barrier, it has to end somewhere."

Tori is appalled. "You mean *ride*? I'm not sure I can stand!"

"Even if we were strong enough to go on," Eli reasons, his face pinched, "we don't know what the barrier will do to us. Farther on it might kill you."

"We could go back," I suggest. "No one has to know we were gone."

"There's a helicopter up there!" Malik argues, holding his head. "We're as easy to spot riding in as riding out!"

"Well, don't blame me!" I snap. "Whose stupid idea was this anyway?"

Tori is distraught. "We can't go on, we can't go back, and we definitely can't stay here! Can anybody think of another option?"

And then something happens—the last thing any of us expect. A woman's voice, not that far away, calls: "Eli . . . !"

We all freeze.

"Who's that?" Hector hisses.

The call comes again. "Eli, are you there . . . ?"

We hear another motor, this one much quieter, and the crunching of tires on the pavement. A car?

We peer out from our hiding place to Old County Six. A dark pickup truck with headlights off is moving slowly east. Every hundred yards or so, it stops, and the woman at the wheel calls for Eli.

Eli begins to step into the open, but Malik grabs him in a hammerlock. "What are you, crazy? Check out the Surety crest on the door. That's a Purple truck!"

The pickup comes to a halt maybe fifty feet away, and the driver calls again. "Eli . . ." This time her face appears in the window.

"It's Mrs. Delaney!" I hiss. "What's she doing here?"

"Her husband's Surety," Malik growls. "Stay down!"

But Eli moves toward the truck in a shambling run. She jumps out of the driver's door and grabs him just as he's about to collapse. "Get in the car. I'll take you home."

"I'm not alone," he manages to say.

That's when she spots the rest of us under the overhang. "I'll take all of you. Put your bikes in the back. Hurry!"

Doing most of the work herself, she hustles us and our stuff into the truck. Without her, I don't think we could have managed it. The agony brought on by the barrier is doing more damage every minute, beating us into the ground.

Malik pauses, holding on to the door of the crew cab. "We're not going back. Take us past this force field, or whatever it is, and we'll be out of your hair."

"It doesn't work that way, Malik," our water polo coach pleads. "The effects get worse before they get better. Your only choice is to go home."

We stare at her a moment, but who would know better

than her? Her husband is a Purple People Eater.

I'm aware of a new pain—one that's just as bad as the pain of this so-called barrier. There's been a lot of crazy talk about Serenity from the other kids. But this is the first time I've heard an adult—a school employee, the wife of a Surety officer—confirm that all is not as it seems in our ideal community.

Eli is bitter. "We have no home. Mrs. Delaney, how much do you know about us?"

"Only what my husband's told me—that some of the kids are part of a study, and that you're not supposed to leave."

"It's worse than that," Eli breathes. "A lot worse."

She's visibly upset. "I knew it was you when Bryan got the call to respond to a perimeter breach. And I also knew I was the only one who could save you. But I'm taking a big risk. If I'm caught, my husband could lose his job, and I could lose my marriage."

Malik jumps on that. "If you turn us in, we'll say the whole thing was your idea."

"Malik!" Tori is horrified. "She's *helping* us!"

He's amazingly cool and steady, despite the waves of pain and nausea. "Then let her help us not get busted."

Mrs. Delaney glares at him, but mostly, she seems

torn. "I don't know *what* the right thing to do is here."

"The right thing is we sneak back home and get up in the morning like this never happened," Malik insists. "You've got just as much to lose as we do."

She puts the engine in gear. "All right," she sighs. "We'll try it your way."

"*Can* we go back?" Hector asks worriedly. "Don't our parents already know?"

"There are false alarms sometimes. The Surety doesn't notify anyone until they rule that out. When the search comes up empty, they'll stand down. You've got to admit that's a better result than any of us deserve." Mrs. Delaney gives Malik a look that would bore a hole into anyone with a thinner skin.

She steps lightly on the gas and we begin to roll, still without headlights, back toward town. We can hear the helicopter, but it's more distant. Through the windshield, we can see the search beam over Old County Six to the west of town.

We haven't gone very far before we begin to feel better—no more nausea; no more headaches. It happens to all of us at virtually the same moment. If there's any doubt that our illness was caused by some kind of unseen barrier, it's gone now. Gone, too, is my belief that Serenity is the place we've always been told it is. My own mother, as our teacher, is one of the main perpetrators of this giant lie. Randy was right all along: something screwy *is* going on in Serenity. Except that the word *screwy* doesn't even begin to describe it. What possible justification could there ever be for people to imprison their own kids with an invisible fence?

"I'm such an idiot!" I mutter.

"No, you're not," Tori says quietly. "You just didn't know."

I'm not consoled. "You tried to tell me, but I wouldn't listen."

Hector turns to her. "Because you were *happy*."

"I'm not happy anymore," I choke.

"Just wait," Malik promises. "You haven't heard the good part yet."

"Enough." Mrs. Delaney pulls onto the shoulder. "This is where everybody gets off. Take your bikes and go home."

"Mrs. Delaney," Eli begins, "I don't know how we can ever thank you—"

"You can't," she interrupts, almost coldly. "This never happened, so there's nothing to be grateful for. I'll keep your secret just this once, because it's my secret too. But

I'm *not* on your side. I'm not on anyone's side, and I intend to keep it that way."

The instant the bikes are unloaded, she drives off without another word.

I face the others, conflicting emotions swirling in my brain, now that the agony has subsided. Heartbreak, embarrassment, fear. Mostly, I feel stupid. I made endless lists, thinking I was in control of my life. And all the while, I didn't have a clue what was going on in the world around me.

And I still don't. "Tell me everything," I urge.

"Not tonight," replies Eli, keeping an anxious eye on the western sky. "Tomorrow. I promise."

I want to argue, but he's right. A helicopter can cover ground a lot faster than a bicycle, and if we're caught, this new reality will be gone before I even understand what it is. Nothing is more important than getting home undetected.

We scatter and I ride up to my door, stash my bike in the garage, and slip into the house. All is quiet; my parents are still asleep. Mrs. Delaney may not be on our side, but she sure was a lifesaver tonight.

The transition from the chaos of the invisible barrier to the familiarity of my much-loved home and my French provincial bedroom is like electric shock therapy. My upright piano; my ballet barre; the color-coded bulletin board where I track my activities. Everything is in perfect order, from my frilly pajamas to my canopy bed.

I refuse to look at it. Everything I thought I understood has just been upended. You might as well repeal the law of gravity, too, so I can't trust that my next step won't send me hurtling off into space.

What is this place where I've spent my whole life? Who are these people who've always been here?

Scariest of all: If I don't know them, do I really know myself?

21
MALIK BRUDER

My mother is the only ballet teacher in Happy Valley, and she has only one student: Laska. Since there aren't any other dancers around, Amber can never be in a real ballet. So every now and then, Mom holds a recital.

I look forward to these recitals with the kind of dread most kids reserve for having their teeth drilled when the dentist from Taos comes to town. About twenty people pack into my living room to see her do pirouettes and grand jetés and a bunch of other stuff with French names. It's about as happening as watching grass die. The only entertainment value is making fun of Amber in a tutu, which never works, since Laska hasn't got the brains to be embarrassed by being seen in a tutu.

Naturally, my mother thinks Amber is the cat's

pajamas. *"Such a lovely girl,"* she always says. Trust me, the night my toe got so swollen that the nail came off and Dad made me soak my foot in salt water for an hour and a half, I wasn't thinking *Such a lovely girl.* But the main reason it drives me nuts that Mom is Laska's number one fan is that the "lovely girl" is just about the polar opposite of me in this place. She takes ballet and piano and volunteers for everything under the sun. For me, it's a point of personal pride to work as little as humanly possible—and even then, I try to con Hector into doing most of it for me. She gets great grades and is a model student, while I just barely squeak by.

The biggest difference between Amber and me is that she's Serenity's biggest fan—a whole cheerleading squad all by herself.

Until now.

On the long day after that very long night, she makes the quickest U-turn in town history. When she reads the web page on Project Osiris, she looks like she's about to eat Eli's iPad in sheer rage.

"Quiet!" Tori advises nervously. "We don't want the Purples on our necks."

So Amber calmly clamps her hands on to the factory fence and squeezes until blood from her fingers begins to trickle along the chain links. Some girls can't handle learning they're clones, I guess. And that other stuff, like your parents being strangers and your entire life being a lie.

It takes all four of us to pull her off the fence. When we let go of her, she sinks into a cross-legged position on the grass. "I want to—" Instead of finishing the sentence, she lashes out a sneakered foot and crushes a grasshopper, twisting it into the ground.

And *I'm* the toxic element? I wonder if anybody ever thought about weeding out Laska.

"How about we just bounce instead?" I suggest.

"Our 'parents'!" she seethes. "They're not going to get away with this!"

The amazing part is that her cheerleading doesn't stop. What's new is that instead of being *for* the town, now she's against it. Suddenly, she hates Happy Valley as much as she loved it before. It almost doesn't matter *how* she feels, just how much.

Hey, I'm not complaining. I'm with her 100 percent. This might be the first thing we've agreed on in thirteen years. Seriously, though, I sympathize with her. The stuff that we've been gradually learning about ourselves over weeks is hitting her all at once. Talk about a shock to the system—especially since a good chunk of it makes about as much sense as *"ARTH   OM W G EN."* In a matter of hours, her entire world has been turned upside down, and most of the details are still a mystery.

"I know you're angry," Eli pleads. "We were just as upset when we found out. But you have to act *normal.* If you start accusing your parents, you'll be giving up the one advantage we have—they don't know that we know."

She's quiet again, but still stubborn. "I don't care."

"The point is," I insist, "here in town, our folks call the shots. Our only chance of having real lives is by busting out. That's what we have to work toward. There's no other way to fight this." The toxic element trying to reason with the ball of fury.

She clenches her jaw. "How about we heave a brick through every window in town? Think they'll get the message then?"

We stare at her in shock. It's so obvious—you're upset, and you lash out and break something. I wonder who she's cloned from. Whoever it is must be someone whose bad side you want to stay away from.

"It's easy to fix a few windows," Hector notes.

Laska's eyes narrow. "How about a whole factory?"

Come to think of it, I'm starting to like her style.

Eli shakes his head. "It doesn't make sense. It would just tip our hand that we're onto them. Then they'd have the five of us on happy pills, not just me. Who knows how long it would take us to figure all this out again, assuming we ever do."

Even Amber has to accept that. She's starting to calm down. I can almost feel her fury morphing into grim determination. "Fine, we escape," she agrees. "But we come back later to get justice for everything that's been done to us."

"If I get out of here," says Hector earnestly, "I'm never coming back. Not even to wreck the place."

"Aren't we getting a little ahead of ourselves?" I ask. "We're not going anywhere until we figure out a way through that invisible fence. Excuse me for taking that a little more personally than the rest of you guys. You know, with Serenity Day coming, and probably Weeding Day right after that."

That shuts everybody up in a hurry. Nothing commands attention like being first on the chopping block. We can't be sure exactly what Project Osiris has in mind for me, but it's hard to imagine it being anything good.

"Well," Tori muses. "What is it about us that we get so sick when we come up against the barrier? Randy didn't.

Our parents don't. And workmen from outside have to pass through it when they come and go. Why aren't they affected?"

"Regular people aren't made in a lab," Eli explains darkly. "When we were born, the scientists must have put something inside us—some kind of antenna or receiver—that reacts to a signal in the barrier. If you don't have the chip or whatever it is, you don't even know the obstacle is there. But if you do—well, just think back to last night."

"Like an invisible dog fence for clones," I put in.

"How can you joke about this?" Amber challenges. "There's something inside us—like a spider crawling around our heads and we can't reach in and get it!"

"It's not alive," Tori soothes.

"It might as well be! It's controlling us, putting a giant wall between us and everywhere else!"

"We're getting too emotional about this," warns Eli. "We have to think like scientists—those are the people who set all this up. The barrier must be some kind of wireless signal—"

"And a wireless signal can be turned off," I finish his thought. "So the trick is to figure out what's generating it."

That becomes Job 1: identifying the source of the

barrier that's keeping us in Happy Valley.

I'm actually kind of optimistic. When the whole town is the size of the average cow pie, there isn't much ground to cover—especially when you consider we're looking for something like an antenna or a transmitter, probably high up. Serenity isn't much *higher* than a cow pie either.

The highest points in town are:

1) The antenna on the roof of the Plastics Works.

2) The clock tower in front of the town hall.

3) The aerial on top of the flagpole in the park.

Using his iPad, Eli takes a picture of all three, and we start checking our photos against similar images online. Turns out that the one on the factory—which I was betting on—is purely a receiver. That must be where the real internet comes from. The web we're allowed to have, plus our TV and radio, all come from Serenity Cable.

The flagpole seems to be a classic cell phone transmitter/receiver, with a very limited range—probably town only. The clock tower is the biggest bust of all. There's nothing up there but clock.

Amber has a brainstorm. "Do you think it could be the Serenity Cup—or maybe the case or the pedestal it stands on?"

I think she might be onto something. Seriously, what other purpose could that hunk of junk serve? It certainly didn't come from Roosevelt, who was dead half a century before Felix Hammerstrom and that billionaire lady got the bright idea to invent Happy Valley.

So the next stop is the park to investigate the Serenity Cup. This is not as easy as it sounds, since Rump L. Stiltskin or some other Purple is sitting in the factory staring at a bunch of video screens, one of which is a live feed from a camera trained right on this wonderful trophy of ours.

Tori comes up with the idea to play Monkey in the Middle so we can fall all over it for a closer look. The Purples may not get a very high opinion of our Frisbee skills, but with any kind of luck, they won't notice that we're searching for hidden antennae and electric wiring, or listening for a power sound.

But here's the thing: turns out the Serenity Cup is about as electric as a loaf of bread. No vibration, no heat, no hum. It's the deadest thing in town, which is saying something when you're talking about Happy Valley.

I channel my disappointment into a vicious tackle on Hector, driving him into the grass with my full weight. I can tell he's really worried about me, because he swallows any word of complaint as he lies there, gasping to regain his breath.

I can't believe it's come to this: I'm being pitied by Hector Amani.

He's limping as we straggle out of the park. "So it's just a trophy?"

"I've got a theory about that," Eli muses. "I think it's kind of an early warning system. The whole purpose of Osiris is to see if we go bad because we're clones of terrible people. So they leave that big silver cup totally unprotected to see which one of us is going to be first to steal it."

"Like I want it," I say sarcastically.

Hector brings us back to earth. "So what do we do? We've eliminated a bunch of things that *aren't* the transmitter, but we still don't know what is."

We hear a familiar roar, and a cone truck drives by on Harmony Street. It's not the one with Hector's blood— I've learned to pick out the crusty brown stains from halfway across town.

And then I see it. I'm pretty sure it's always been there, but there's so much to question about the cargo that we never bothered to look at the truck itself. There is a small rotating satellite dish about two feet in diameter on the roof of the cab.

I pinch Eli hard. "Ow!"

"Do the other trucks have those?"

He rubs his arm, scowling. "I don't think so."

"The one I bled on definitely doesn't," puts in Hector.

Amber speaks up. "I always figured it was, like, a GPS or something."

"Why would you need a GPS on a truck that rides around in circles and never leaves town?" asks Eli.

I grin. "You wouldn't. Unless your GPS isn't a GPS."

22
ELI FRIEDEN

Of the four cars ahead of me, the blue one is the problem. It's weaving into the gap every time I try to pass. I yank on the wheel in an attempt to sneak through on the inside, but my tire scrapes against the curb and I have to veer off.

Suddenly, the blue car spins out on the straightaway. I jump into the empty space, threading the needle between the green SUV and the yellow taxi. A victorious cry of "Yes!" escapes me. I'm in second place.

My father appears in the doorway. "Eli, isn't it about time you started your homework?"

Who can think about homework now? I've only got one more racer to beat!

My foot presses down where the gas pedal would be

if this was a real car. I jump past the red convertible into the lead.

"Eli?" Louder this time. "You've been at this for a couple of hours already. There's nothing wrong with a little gaming, but when did you become such a 'vidiot'?"

There's an answer to that question, but not one I can give to Dad.

I'm teaching myself how to drive.

Sure, I know that there's a big difference between *Street Racers 2014* and actually being behind the wheel of a motor vehicle. But this is the closest I'm going to get, and it'll have to do. At least the steering part is kind of similar, and the way the road comes at you. I'll have to get the hang of the gas and brake pedals on the fly. Malik is doing the same thing on his own game system.

I pause the Xbox. "You're right, Dad. I'll get to it."

I've been very obedient lately. We all have. Our obedience is part of the plan to pave the way for the colossal act of disobedience that's coming up soon.

"Good work habits take a lifetime to develop," Dad lectures. "Poor ones take barely a heartbeat."

More life lessons from the guy who cloned criminals just to see what would happen.

I try to seem abashed. "Sorry."

He softens. "Don't be too hard on yourself. Serenity Day is coming up. We all feel the spirit in the air."

Yeah, Dad, you just said a mouthful.

"I have something to show you, Eli. I thought you might know who this belongs to."

I recognize it before he even turns over the three-by-five card. He hands it to me. It's Baron Vladimir von Horseteeth, one of everybody's favorites. I can tell by its dog-eared condition that it's changed hands more than a few times around school.

"Where did you get it?" I ask in a small voice.

"Mrs. Laska found it after Meditation today. I recognize Randy's handwriting. And maybe one that's a little more familiar . . ."

My mind whirls. This is the worst possible time for Dad to get suspicious. Better to make a full confession and take my lumps than risk having him think I'm hiding something.

"There's a whole set," I admit, my ears burning. "The kids trade them. We didn't mean any harm."

"It's disrespectful of the good work the Surety does for us," my father says with a disapproving frown.

"I know. We made them as a joke and they just kind of

caught on. I take all the blame."

"Oh, I'm giving you all the blame," he says. "Randy isn't here to share any of it with you." Then he does something completely unexpected. He laughs at his own joke. This blows me away because a) he laughed, and b) he made a joke.

Of course, he does tear up the Baron. "I expect you to do the same with the others as soon as you collect them." And he walks out of the room. But I can see that he is trying hard not to smile. Unbelievable! Either my father has a sense of humor, or the Purple People Eaters are even more goof-worthy than Randy and I thought.

I wait until he's all the way down to the kitchen before resuming my game, this time with the sound muted. Driving lessons aren't an option; they're a necessity. It's Tori's idea. She's the one who came to the conclusion that if we're going to escape Serenity, bikes just won't cut it. Look how fast Mrs. Delaney made it out to where we rode that night.

"By the time our parents realize we're missing and send the Purples after us, we need to be far enough away that they won't know where to look. Face it, we're going to have to be in a car."

We've even figured out which car we're going to be

taking—my dad's brand-new Lexus. It'll be easy. He leaves the spare keys in the junk drawer in our kitchen. Why would he bother to hide them? The only potential car thieves in town can't make it past the invisible fence.

Or so he thinks.

Knowing that the barrier is being generated by the satellite dish on that cone truck changes everything. True, we can't be 100 percent positive until we test it, but we've scoured the town, and there's nothing else it could possibly be.

The plan is simplicity itself: knock out the dish, take the car, and good-bye.

By the time Malik and I feel even semiconfident behind the wheel, Serenity Day is less than forty-eight hours away.

I'm nervous. "It's too risky to try anything now. People are outside, decorating their houses with streamers and bunting. The Purples are all over the park, setting up the picnic tables."

"Maybe we should wait a few days," Amber suggests. "You know, till after the celebration is over."

"That's easy for you to say," protests Hector. "The minute Serenity Day is done, Malik might get weeded. They could send him away, and we'll never see him again!

For all we know, it means . . ." He falls silent.

"Chill out, Hector," Malik says quietly. "It's supposed to happen after Serenity Day, but not necessarily in the first five minutes after. I'll be fine." He's trying to sound confident, and not really succeeding.

"Or," Tori interjects, "we could make our move on Serenity Day itself, right in the middle of the nighttime fireworks."

We goggle at her.

"It's the perfect distraction," she insists. "The whole town's in the park. Even the Purple People Eaters are on skeleton staff. It's dark, and everybody's eating ice cream and looking up."

"I take back every time I called you stupid!" Malik crows. "Serenity Day! Like we're taking their un-holiday and using it against them!" There's genuine relief beneath the surface of his usual in-your-face attitude.

"Don't celebrate yet," I warn. "There are a million things that can go wrong, and some of them probably will. We have to know this plan like the back of our hands and get every single detail exactly right."

In a town full of well-behaved kids, we make sure we're the best behaved of the lot. You can practically see our halos. We go to school, put the finishing touches on our Serenity Day projects, and practice in the pool for the big water polo match. But in private, when nobody's watching, we spend every spare minute reading up on life in the real world. We save our allowances, open old piggy banks, and hoard every dollar offered to us to buy a snack or ice cream cone. Not even Tori can plan more than a few miles past the town limits, because none of us has any idea what we'll find out there. Will a group of kids on their own attract attention? Where can we live and sleep? How important will money be? Will Osiris send the Purple People Eaters to track us down, or will they write us off and focus on the clones they have left?

"They have to come after us," is Amber's opinion. "We're walking, talking proof of what they've being doing in Serenity—what they're *still* doing."

"What if the outside world already knows about Project Osiris and thinks it's just fine?" Tori muses.

Hector shakes his head. "Not according to the internet. That website says Osiris was scrapped because it was considered immoral. I think our folks would be in big trouble if word gets out about us."

"I'm counting on it," Amber says. "I want to be there to see my parents' faces when I testify against them in court. I hope they go to jail for what they did."

The rest of us exchange uncomfortable glances. Although we're all angry with our parents, Amber's desire for revenge is a little chilling. I can't help but wonder whose DNA she wound up with. My father deserves to be brought to justice more than anybody, yet it hurts to think of him suffering in some jail.

Not only is our plan half-baked; we're not even sure what to hope for if we succeed.

Another possible weakness is Mrs. Delaney. She knows what we tried to do that night. She's kept our secret so far—if she hadn't, we'd all be on Dr. Bruder's magic pills. But she's in a tough spot herself, being married to a Purple People Eater. And as our water polo coach, she sees us every day, which gives her plenty of chances to ponder whether or not she's doing the right thing by covering for us.

We're all swimming extra hard to keep her happy. The quality of water polo in this town has never been better. I think she sees through it, though. She's been distant and all business where she used to be warm and friendly. I try to engage her in conversation a few times, but she only wants to talk about improving our skills.

Once, in private, I even go so far as to mention ". . . the time you gave us a lift in that Surety pickup."

She doesn't take the bait.

"We don't need her to sign a blood oath, Eli," Malik points out. "We just need her to keep her mouth shut a few more days."

"Besides," adds Tori, "it's not like she's the only thing that can go wrong. Face it, the minute we're past the barrier, we're lost. We haven't got a clue where we're going and there's nobody we can ask, since we don't know a single person outside Serenity."

"That's not technically true." I actually thought of this a couple of days ago, but I haven't mentioned anything before now, because I'm still not sure if it's worth pursuing. But with the time to zero hour counting down, it's something we all have to consider. "We *do* know someone out there. We know Randy Hardaway."

23

AMBER LASKA

Last year on the eve of Serenity Day, I was so excited that I didn't sleep. I was going to get my face painted and eat cotton candy until I threw up on the Fun Slide or the Bouncy Castle. I was going to drink real soda, which Mom never keeps in the house. It was all bogus, yet it still makes me a little sad to think that I'm probably never going to be that psyched about anything again.

My to-do list from that day is still pinned to my corkboard. It's unique because of what's *not* on it—no ballet or piano practice, no homework, or anything to do with school:

- Go on Rides
- Win Three-Legged Race with Tori

- Listen (!!!) to Speeches
- Present Project
- The Big Game
- Cheer for Dad in Plastics-Works-versus-
  Surety Tug-of-War
- Fireworks

What a difference a year makes.

This time around, I don't get much sleep either, but for a reason that has nothing to do with cotton candy or water polo. I'm still looking forward to the fireworks, but not to ooh and aah over the explosions of color. And there's no list at all. The last thing I want to do is put our plan in writing and pin it to my corkboard where Mom and Dad can see it. Anyway, it would be a very short list:

- Don't blow it.

It's as if my entire body is a guitar string, vibrating with nervous determination. Today is the most important day of my life. And if it goes well, tomorrow will be the first day of a new one.

It starts in the afternoon with family picnics in the park. Family—I don't even know what that word means anymore. Tori has told me at least twenty times that my parents love me. I don't deny that they were nice to me for thirteen years and gave me a cushy life. Everybody has a cushy life here, not from any plastics factory, or community philosophy, but because some billionaire coughed up tons of money to create a whole town and turn it into a giant behavior lab.

So, yeah, maybe they love me, but that's beside the point. They lied to me, all the while claiming that nothing is more important than honesty. I've been pumped up with so many lies that when you take them away, there's nothing left and I'm an empty shell. I'll never forgive them for that.

I've done my share of crying; now it's time to move on. I guess the criminal mastermind I'm cloned from isn't the sentimental type.

The ceremony starts at around two, when Mr. Frieden holds up the Serenity Cup and we all go nuts for about ten minutes, applauding, hugging our neighbors, shaking hands, and pounding people on the back. I lock eyes with Tori. She's red-faced from cheering her head off, and I'm sure I am too. We're determined to be the most enthusiastic Serenity citizens of them all—until tonight, when we vote with our feet.

The speeches are the same as always, but this is the first year I find them painful to the ears. The speakers are introduced by their fancy titles: Mayor; CEO of the Plastics Works; Chief Medical Officer; Chamber of Commerce President. But in reality, these are our parents and neighbors, people we've seen in bathing suits and in line at the store buying Metamucil. I fell for it harder than most of the kids and I'm not proud of that. It only strengthens my resolve. I won't be their stooge anymore.

Then the "fun" begins. I allow myself a few jumps in the Bouncy Castle and some cotton candy for old times' sake. For the egg-and-spoon race, Mrs. Amani hands me a soup ladle deep enough to float the *Queen Mary*, and I speak up and ask for the same regular spoon everyone else has. The adults nod approvingly. Now I understand I've passed another test. But what's most satisfying to me is that by the time they get the chance to note it on my whiteboard, I'll be gone.

Next it's on to the school for the presentation of our projects. Tori and I win first prize. I can't take much credit for that. Tori's the artist; my contribution is basically smearing blue on the sky and green on the grass. We're awarded plaques we can hang in the rooms we're not going to live in anymore.

Then it's time for the water polo match, Team Solidarity against Team Community. The whole town packs into the bleachers around the natatorium. There are even some Purple People Eaters among the spectators. This is the one day of the year that they actually mingle.

As we stand at attention for the national anthem and "Serenity, My Home," my mind wanders to the sports pages of that *USA Today*. There was coverage of baseball, football, basketball, hockey, soccer, tennis, lacrosse, and any sport you can imagine. But not a word about water polo. Why is it so popular here? Is Project Osiris monitoring our aggressive and competitive tendencies in an environment where we're surrounded by water and insulated from major injury?

Clones must be expensive.

The game is a blur of splashing and yelling, the ball whizzing past my head, first in one direction, then the other. It's hard to care about athletic glory when you've got so much going on soon. Even Malik is a subdued version of his usual Zeus-hurling-thunderbolts self. The match ends 4–4. The audience goes wild. In Serenity, we love ties because nobody goes home disappointed. That's harmony and contentment for you. As for honesty . . . two out of three ain't bad.

By the time we get changed and back to the park, the barbecues are blazing and the sun is low in the sky. My last Serenity sunset. I should be happy, but I'm starting to get really scared. My eyes seek out the others in the crowd, and I can tell they're thinking the same thing. We're heart-and-soul behind this plan, but it's about to get very real very fast.

The Purple People Eaters lose the Plastics-Works-versus-Surety tug-of-war. They lose on purpose—they always do to show what great sports they are. It's nice to see those perfect purple uniforms dragged through the mud and slime of the pit, but I'm too anxious to enjoy it. The waiting is torture and the hard part—the escape—hasn't even started yet. I'm having trouble wrapping my mind around the enormity of what we're about to do.

A hot dog is waved under my nose. "Eat something, honey," my mother exhorts. "You must be starving."

I have such a nervous stomach that the smell of it almost makes me retch. "I'm not really hungry."

"After all that swimming?"

So I take a bite and choke it down just to avoid an argument, or, worse, her taking me home for a little TLC. It's gross but I can't shake the feeling that it's not going to be the worst thing I have to do tonight.

The sun is down. Dusk is quickly turning to darkness. The fireworks are about to begin.

In more ways than one.

24

ELI FRIEDEN

It's easy to slip out of the park. Everybody's eyes are on the fireworks.

Malik and I dart into the trees and pause for a moment to make sure we're not being followed. We haven't got much time to waste, though. I have it on the highest authority—Dad's—that this year's Serenity Day extravaganza will last exactly twenty-three minutes.

"Clear," whispers Malik, and we're off.

In some bushes at the corner of the park, we've stashed the closest thing we could get to demolition tools—a shovel and a hoe from Dr. Bruder's backyard shed. I'd feel a lot surer of success with a sledgehammer and dynamite, but that kind of stuff is hard to come by in this town. Anyway, beggars can't be choosers.

The streets are deserted, so we have no trouble winding up at the foot of the Fellowship hill. We peer through the factory gate. There they are, parked just inside—the three cone trucks. The one with the satellite dish is in the middle.

"Looks like it's wearing a crown," I mumble.

Malik grimaces. "Let's dethrone it."

There's no sign of the Surety patrol. Maybe it doesn't even operate on Serenity Day. The Purple People Eaters have other jobs tonight, like setting off fireworks and losing the tug-of-war.

Tools in hand, we scale the fence and run to the center truck. I hoist myself onto the hood and Malik climbs aboard via the payload, kicking dusty cones in all directions. We reach the dish at the same instant.

"Remember," I breathe, "try to time the blows with the explosions of the skyrockets. That way, there's less chance anyone will hear us."

"Yeah, you do that," he tells me. "I've waited thirteen years to beat the snot out of something, and I'm planning to do a good job."

He means it, too, because his first swing with the hoe misses the end of my nose by about three inches. It makes a gonging sound as it slams into the metal dish, denting it.

I start whacking away with my shovel, all the while searching for some cable to cut. I've brought our meat scissors, which would behead a rhino. But the signal generator is stronger than it looks, and the wiring must be inside it. We're inflicting major damage on the dish, twisting it into a piece of modern art. Shards are breaking off and flying every which way. Yet the heavy base of the thing is almost untouched.

I change my strategy, leaving the hacking to Malik, and concentrating on trying to break the connection between the control box and the truck body. I pound on the roof of the cab in an attempt to buckle it. If I can create a little space, maybe I can get my shovel underneath and lever it off. Then I can slice through the wires, get it on the ground, and Malik and I can pound it into jelly.

Perspiration is pouring off Malik, and he grunts with every swing of the hoe. I must be just as bad, because my eyes are stinging, and I'm having trouble with my grip on the shovel—that's how sweaty my hands are. We battle on furiously. All this as detonations of light and color go off in the sky over our heads.

That might explain why we never hear the golf cart.

"Freeze!" booms a deep voice.

The next thing I know, a purple arm has Malik in a

headlock, and I realize we've been caught. His eyes widen in terror, but he's unable to struggle or even cry out.

Without even thinking, I swing my shovel around and catch Alexander the Grape right between the shoulder blades. He drops like a stone and rolls off onto the ground, where he lies still, gasping for breath. That's when I see the cart parked behind us. Bryan Delaney is out and running toward us, his expression full of fury.

"Hang on!" I yell at Malik, who is dazed but unhurt.

And just like I know what I'm doing, I abandon the shovel and vault into the cab of the truck. There's no key in the ignition, but I flip the sun visor, and the key falls into my lap. I jam it into the slot and twist. The big engine roars to life. Desperately, I take in my surroundings and realize in horror that this is nothing like *Street Racers 2014*. The transmission is a stick shift. I've read about these in books, but since Dad's Lexus is automatic, I never bothered to research how to drive one.

I give it some gas, forcing the handle into the spot marked 1. There's an awful screech, and the truck shudders but doesn't go anywhere.

"The clutch!" hollers Malik. "Use the clutch!"

"I'm clutching it as hard as I can!" I shout back.

"It's the pedal! To the left of the brake!"

Clearly, Malik has a more realistic video game than mine. I press down on the clutch and reshift, and this time the truck begins to crawl out from between its brothers. There's a thump as Bryan jumps on my running board. An indigo-sleeved arm reaches in for me. The hand grabs my hair. It hurts, but it gives me time to roll up the window, catching him just below the elbow. Out of the corner of my eye, I see the hoe handle come around and whack him on the side of the head. His body stiffens, and I lower the window just enough to allow him to fall off.

"Go, go, go!" orders Malik.

"Get in the truck with me!" I shout back.

"I can't. I'm busy!"

I can hear him still hacking at the dish on the roof. He's right. All of this is for nothing if we can't knock out the barrier.

The cone truck plows through the metal gate, leaving a snarl of broken and twisted chain behind it. I wheel onto Fellowship Avenue and shift into second for going up the hill. There's another screech, and for an awful moment the motor begins to cough and sputter.

Don't stall . . . please don't stall, I beg silently.

In the rearview mirror, I see the golf cart with the two Purple People Eaters working its way through the ruined gate. They make the turn onto Fellowship and start after us. Bryan is bleeding from the side of his face. I swallow an involuntary wheeze. It's the first time I've ever drawn blood from another person.

Sorry, Mrs. Delaney.

"Drive!" howls Malik in between loud blows.

It hits me in a stab of panic that if the engine dies, I have no idea how to get it started again. It's putt-putt-putting dangerously slow, and then it catches with a smooth healthy sound. We crest the hill and I head for the park, ignoring stop signs. The fireworks display is still going on, which means we're not too late.

The golf cart is just fast enough to keep pace, or maybe I'm slow enough to keep pace with it. The truck can do better, but not in this gear, and I don't dare shift into third. I came perilously close to stalling before. I'm not taking that risk again.

The park is dead ahead of us on the left. "I see them!" Malik calls from the roof.

I do too—Hector and the girls, by the mayor's parking space, where Dad left the Lexus. The surveillance camera that monitors this part of town is at their feet in several pieces—Tori's job. They're waiting for Malik and me to come running back so we can pile into the car and take off. Now, though, we're in the truck, not on foot. And with two Purples chasing us, there's no time to switch vehicles.

At the sight of the factory truck, the three try to melt into the shadows.

"It's us, you morons!" Malik stage-whispers. "Get on—now! Change of plan—we're not stopping!"

The instruction bewilders them at first, even after they see who's driving. Then they spot the golf cart coming up behind us, and they're spurred into action. Hector and Amber clamber onto the back, joining Malik among the cones. Tori jumps into the cab with me.

In the sky above us, seven big rockets splay out in a cascade of red, white, and blue. It's the beginning of the grand finale. Our twenty-three minutes are almost up.

"Can't this thing go any faster?" Tori asks anxiously.

Mentally crossing my fingers, toes, and heart, I depress the clutch and shift into third.

There's a bit of a screech, and the truck bucks once, but the engine is running smoothly and we take off. I stomp on the gas and we surge ahead. The golf cart grows smaller in the mirror as the speedometer climbs past twenty, thirty, and even forty.

Cheering comes from the back of the truck, Hector

and Amber celebrating our leaving the patrol in the dust.

"They'll never catch us now!" Amber exults.

But it'll be a pretty short-lived victory if we haven't taken out the barrier.

The cab resonates with the crack of Malik's hoe against the dish. He's thinking what I'm thinking. The signal generator is bent and broken, not to mention beaten to a pulp. But we haven't been able to get at the guts. Our only hope is that the damage to the outside is enough to mess up the works.

I take the turn onto Old County Six so fast that I send four or five orange cones flying out of the payload and skittering across the grass.

"Slow down!" howls Hector. "I can't hang on!"

"Slow down?" Malik barks. "Speed up!"

That we definitely are. The speedometer is inching past sixty and I'm starting to feel a little more in control behind the wheel. The *Now Leaving Serenity* sign is upon us and past almost before we think to look for it. Town is gone except for a few sparks from the end of the fireworks. And it's only a matter of time before it begins to sink in that so are we.

"So far, so good," says Tori in a small voice.

"I'm good too." Actually, I ache all over, but that's the

tension in my arms and shoulders from hanging on to this big wheel. I don't dare take my eyes off the road, but I'm pretty sure we're getting to the point where the barrier would start acting on us—if the barrier is still in operation.

A whimper from Amber reaches me through the open window, and by the time I process what that might mean, I feel it too—the nauseated stomach, the pain and pressure in my head.

Oh no! The barrier—it's still there!

The onset is sudden and overwhelming—a blinding, searing agony that grips our entire bodies, blotting out everything else.

It's our speed, I think, struggling to maintain control of the truck. *We're not on bikes this time; we're blasting into the heart of the barrier at sixty miles per hour!*

Tori is half out of her seat, doubled over and retching. Above me I hear Malik hacking furiously at the dish in a last-ditch effort to destroy it before it destroys us. Hector is screaming; Amber is moaning. It's a nightmare moment of total chaos, but even worse than our suffering is the crushing reality that we've lost. The choice we face is grim in the extreme: We can turn around and be dragged back to live the rest of our lives as prisoners and lab rats. Or we can go forward and die.

Total failure. We were in such a hurry to get Malik out of town by Serenity Day that we patched together a plan without really thinking it through. How could we be so crazy as to believe that we could knock out a sophisticated high-tech barrier system with *gardening tools?* Even now, through the waves of nausea and torture, I hear the *whack, whack, whack* of Malik relentlessly pummeling the dish, never giving up, although the hoe in his hand is inadequate to get the job done.

He fights valiantly on. The hoe may be puny, but it's the only weapon we've got . . .

All at once, through the fog that's coming down over my eyes, it dawns on me that we *do* have another weapon.

We have a speeding truck!

I scream at Tori, "Get me an orange cone!"

She's so lost in her misery that it takes a few seconds before she realizes I'm talking to her.

I scream again. "A cone! Now!"

Moving like a ninety-year-old, she eases her upper body out the window. There's some shouted conversation over the engine noise, and when she comes back into the cab, she's holding out a traffic cone. I take it and scan the road ahead in the high beams. To my right is a deepening valley; on the left, desert pines announce the edge of the Carson National Forest.

"Get ready to jump," I tell Tori.

"What? Jump? Why?"

There's no time for an explanation, because up ahead the lights illuminate exactly what I was looking for. A weather-beaten sign warns of a sharp left turn directly ahead. Just beyond it, a line of white-painted wooden posts follow the curve of the road.

I grab the cone and jam it into the gas pedal, wedging it against the front of my seat. The truck surges forward, the speedometer leaping past seventy.

"Now!" I bark at Tori.

With a terrified cry, she throws open the passenger door and hurls herself out. I try to make sure that she's clear of the giant tires, but she's already far behind, and whatever happened, happened.

Still keeping one hand on the wheel, I open my own door and step out onto the running board. "Jump!" I howl at the three in the payload. "Do it! Now!"

At this speed, the simple act of dropping from the truck is like being hurled violently backward. I count two jumpers not three. The smallest figure is still there—Hector, frozen in fear, hanging on to the mesh gate at the rear.

"Hector, ju-u-ump!!"

I can't be sure if he goes or not, because at that instant, I'm out of time. The warning sign flashes past. The white-painted posts are hurtling toward me; beyond them lies the drop into the valley. It's now or never.

I fling myself into the night. I feel the pull of the slip-stream as the truck barrels past. My momentum carries me to a gravelly shoulder, and I'm slammed down as if by a giant hand. I look up just in time to see the cone truck bashing through the line of posts and sailing over the precipice. It has a rough ride. I can hear it bouncing off boulders and crashing through underbrush, taking out trees. I've lost sight of it now, but I know when it hits bottom. An enormous explosion rocks the countryside, and a huge fireball rises up into the sky, momentarily turning the valley bright as high noon.

This is our *Serenity Day fireworks,* I think to myself with a stab of savage satisfaction. They definitely saw it from town. It was probably visible from the International Space Station.

I am scraped and bruised and bleeding all over. Everything hurts, and yet for some reason, I feel terrific.

It takes a moment before I realize why. The paralyzing headache and nausea are gone. When the truck blew up, it took the barrier generator with it.

A rush of exhilaration comes over me. The walls of our prison were never brick and mortar, but they were just as real. For the first time in our lives, we're free.

We. The word snaps my mind back to the others. I hope they're okay. I made it, so surely they did, too, didn't they?

My sense of triumph goes cold as I think of Hector. Did he get off in time? And even if he did, a lot can go wrong jumping from a vehicle moving at seventy miles an hour. You could break bones; you could slip under the wheels; you could hit your head on a rock.

"Hector!" I call. "Tori! Amber! Malik!"

The names echo in the stillness.

My blood turns cold. Am I the only one alive?

By the time my body hits the shoulder, the speeding truck is already thirty feet past. The impact is bone-splitting. I try to see what's happening with the others, but I'm already rolling, and the whole world is a blur. I hear some-one screaming and I'm pretty sure it's me.

Through the whirling kaleidoscope of dark land and sky, I catch a glimpse of the yawning valley growing closer. If I go over the side, I'm dead for sure. Desperately, I reach out to grab something—anything—to stop my momentum. My fingers dig into dirt and dry grass, but it all comes away in my hands.

Try harder! I exhort myself. *It's a long way down!*

My arms clamp around a prickly bush. Thorns pierce into my skin, but I hang on through the barrage of pain.

Who knew that life is so precious? Who knew?

When I finally stop moving, I have only a split second to celebrate my narrow escape. A half mile ahead, the cone truck smashes through the white fence posts and hurtles over the edge. My breath catches in my throat as I hear it tumbling all the way down. I see the fireball slightly before I hear the noise of the explosion, and I can't help but think of Amber's mom, who taught us how light travels faster than sound.

The others, I think with a gasp of horror. I jumped; did anybody else? If they didn't, there's no way they could have survived.

The pain and nausea of the barrier are gone now. We were right—it was the dish on the truck. It's small comfort in my present situation.

I struggle up, which is no small thing when you're broken to pieces. There might be a couple of tiny hair follicles that don't hurt; everything else is killing me. Tears are running down my face, not only for the fate of my poor friends, but also for myself, because what if I'm all alone out here?

"Amber!" I call. "Eli! Malik! Hector!" My voice is raw, and thin as tracing paper. No one can hear me. The sound probably doesn't carry more than a few feet.

I limp along the road, enduring a symphony of pain. I was the first to jump. If anybody else made it, too, that's where they'll be. It isn't far, but my ankle is on fire. I must have sprained it when I hit the ground. Out of the corner of my eye, I catch a hint of movement, and my heart leaps.

"Amber?"

But it isn't Amber. It isn't anybody. Distant lights from the direction of Serenity. Cars coming to investigate the big explosion.

Purple People Eaters! Or worse, our parents!

Parents! Suddenly, I feel the need to wrap my bruised body in Dad's embrace. He'll forgive me and tell me everything's fine. That picture is so achingly tempting it nearly tears me in two. This nightmare can be over soon. He'll be here in just a few minutes. All I have to do is wait. For sure he's in the first car . . .

No! I shake my head as hard as I can. It sets off a firestorm of pain, but it's worth it to clear my mind. Dad's comfort is a lie. *Dad* is a lie! Our parents are on the other side and I can't let them catch me.

The thought urges me into action. I scramble for the woods. I'm abandoning my search for the others. But it stands to reason that any survivors will see those same headlights and run for cover too.

I pound through the forest, sidestepping tree trunks and tripping over exposed roots. As the overhead foliage thickens into a canopy, the light of the moon and stars is lost, and I'm stumbling blind. As I flee, the logical part of my brain is screaming: *Turn around before you knock yourself unconscious and never wake up again because some rattlesnake or coyote eats you!*

Then I think about my life as a prisoner and a clone, and the rattlesnakes and coyotes don't seem that bad.

My eyes are just beginning to adjust to the low light when the collision comes. I bounce off, the wind knocked out of me. It's so devastating that I'm positive I've run full tilt into a tree.

But trees don't curse, and this one does.

"Malik!" I rasp, grabbing on to him. "Don't leave! It's me! Tori!"

"Tori!" Amber's voice.

We all start babbling at the same time until Malik suddenly interrupts. "Where's Hector?"

"I don't know." I'm brought up short. "I thought I was the only one who made it until I found you guys. What about Eli?"

"When we jumped, he was still standing on the running board, steering," Amber supplies breathlessly.

"Eli can take care of himself," Malik snaps. "We've got to look for the shrimp!"

I shake my head. "We can't. There's a parade of cars coming up from Serenity."

"We'll find him quick and then get out of here," Malik says stubbornly.

We form a search line, fanning out about ten feet apart. We don't dare go any farther than that for fear of losing each other.

We haven't made much progress when a faint voice echoes through the woods. We practically have to tackle Malik to keep him from running off on his own.

I call, "Over here!" but I'm still incapable of much sound.

Not Malik, though. He has no problem mustering top volume while struggling to break free of our grip. *"Hector!!"*

There's rustling in the underbrush, and a figure joins us in the gloom. "It's me," says Eli.

Eli! I thought I'd never see him again. "We're all here except Hector," I quaver.

There's a tremor in his voice. "I don't know about Hector. I begged him to jump, but I think he was too scared. I don't know if he got off the truck in time."

His words are quiet, but their impact is greater than the shock wave that came with the fireball. We've obviously always understood that our plan was dangerous, and that not all of us might survive it. Now we have to deal with the fact that it might have already happened—that Hector went over the side with the truck.

We knew there'd be a price for our freedom. But we never expected Hector to pay it for the rest of us.

"Stupid Hector!" Malik's chest begins to heave. "Leave it to him to screw up so bad! He couldn't manage one little thing to save his worthless life! How hard is it to fall off a truck you can barely hang on to in the first place?"

"He did his best, Malik," I offer gently. "He just froze up. He must have been really terrified."

"He's useless!" Malik raves. "Who did they clone him from—a baboon? And when he really needed me"—his voice catches in his throat—"*I wasn't there!*"

We stand in mute astonishment. Malik, who doesn't care about anything or anybody, is *crying*! He covers his scratched face with his hands, but still the tears drip through his fingers, mingling with dirt and blood. Amber reaches down to place a comforting hand on his shoulder, but he shakes her off.

A loud, rhythmic clatter swells out of the background.

I've been hearing it for a while, but in the chaos of the moment, it doesn't really penetrate my thoughts until this minute.

"A helicopter," I breathe. Then, "Purples!"

Our break for freedom has come to disaster. One of us is probably dead, and now the Surety is swooping down to pick us up.

"Run!" rasps Eli.

We take off like a herd of wild horses, deeper into the woods. We haven't gone very far when the engine roar swells directly overhead. The searchlight beam sweeps over the trees not fifty feet away from us, so close that we're sure we must be discovered. But the chopper continues on, coming to hover just beyond the ridge where the road curves. Slowly, it begins to descend into the valley.

"They didn't see us," I whisper.

Eli clues in. "The truck's at the bottom of the slope, on fire. That's what's drawing their attention. They probably think they're going to find five bodies in there."

Malik is still emotional. "They *are* going to find *one* body in there."

"Listen, Malik," Eli says earnestly. "Whatever happened to Hector, hanging around here is only going to get us caught."

"And *I'm* supposed to be the toxic element?" Malik spits. "At least I'm not stone cold like you! I'll bet they had to go pretty deep into the psycho ward to find *your* DNA! No wonder the ringleader of Osiris picked you to raise."

Eli recoils as if he's been slapped, but he doesn't give up on his argument. "This is a *gift*," he persists. "That truck is going to burn for a while before they can get close enough to see that we're not all in it. By the time it cools off enough for them to investigate, we have to be a long way from here."

"I guess I was wrong about you, Hector," Malik rasps aloud. "You're not useless after all. You're useful as one thing—a distraction. That's what your whole life was about."

"Come on, Malik. It won't help Hector if we get dragged back to Serenity." Amber touches his arm.

Malik takes a shaky breath. "Nothing can help Hector now."

"Where are we going to go?" I wonder, my entire body trembling. "I mean, with the car we could head for Taos or some other town, but now we're on foot. We can't walk eighty miles—not with the Purples looking for us. No truck burns *that* long."

Eli's ready with an answer. "The train line. That was

our plan when we tried to get away on our bikes. There's no reason why we can't put that into action now. If we keep heading south, we know we'll hit the tracks eventually."

"Yeah, but *how* eventually?" Amber asks. "It has to be miles, probably a lot of them."

We turn to Malik, who is still mourning. He looks like he couldn't put one foot in front of the other, much less take on a marathon backcountry hike in the dark.

His grief-stricken features twist into a slight smile. "You've got someplace else you need to be?"

26

MALIK BRUDER

I always thought Serenity was the lamest backwater on the face of the earth. Now I know that compared with what's *around* Serenity, the town itself is New York or Paris or Tokyo or one of those huge cities you read about.

What's around Serenity is basically nothing. I know this because we walk through every lousy inch of it. It's dirt and trees and sagebrush that grabs at your feet and ankles. It's boulders and buttes and crags that have to be scrambled over or squeezed between. It's so quiet that the only sound besides your own groaning and cursing is the scampering of lizards or the clicking of scorpions. Poor Hector would have probably wet himself, but come to think of it, he'd be too dehydrated, like the rest of us.

It would be hard enough to keep going under any

296

circumstances, but after what we've just been through, it's torture in the extreme. We walk all night, blundering through darkness, until the pain of our exhaustion equals the pain of the cuts and bruises that cover 99 percent of our bodies. I'd probably be carrying Hector by now. Under the circumstances, I'd be happy to do it. He doesn't weigh very much.

Correction: He *didn't* . . .

Here's what haunts me: If we didn't have to rush our plan in order to get *me* out of Happy Valley before Weeding Day, could we have come up with a better way to do it that didn't get Hector killed? If I didn't cheat on tests and gorge myself on cookies and cupcakes and get myself classified "toxic"; if I wasn't such a big *jerk*, would Hector still be alive?

That's a lot more weight to carry than one skinny kid.

The girls are tougher than I thought. I figured they'd be flat on their faces at this point, but they're hanging in there. I guess when it's your only chance to have a real life, you keep putting one foot in front of the other, regardless of how much it hurts. That goes double when you're the one on full weeding alert. I don't feel very lucky, but I understand I am. If we didn't get out when we did, who knows what would have happened to me.

I don't know how far we've come, but we can't see or hear the helicopter anymore. Maybe it landed in the valley, or maybe the Purples took it back to base to wait for first light. I'm hoping that we've walked clear out of its range. I've got the blisters on my feet to prove it.

Our navigation can be summed up in one word: south. We think we're heading in the right direction, but it's easy to get turned around when you're traveling over rough terrain. It feels like we've been on the move for about six months when, at last, the disk of the sun eases its way over the horizon and we're heading straight for it.

"We're going *east!*" wails Tori.

That's the only word of complaint. We make our course correction, but we're too tired for much more grumbling. We're thirsty and we're hungry. When the sun climbs, it begins to pound down on us unmercifully.

"You know, when they picked a place for their secret clone farm, they really scored," I pant. "We've been walking for, like, fifteen hours and we haven't seen a single person. Not even a house or a road or a power line."

"Be grateful," Eli grunts. "We could be seeing lots of people—in purple suits."

I'm sweating like crazy, but that's a sign that, so far, I'm still okay. I heard once that it's when you stop sweating that you know the dehydration is getting really bad.

"It's so hot!" Tori exclaims.

"No hotter than Happy Valley," I point out.

"Yeah, but there, you're never far from air-conditioning or a pool," Amber complains.

I wish I had my pool right now. I'd drink it, chlorine and all.

"I give our parents credit for one thing," I offer. "They kept us pampered while we were under their microscope."

"I'll take this over all their toys and comforts," Eli says through gritted teeth. "At least I'm nobody's lab rat."

I'm down with that, but a nervous thought has begun to nag at me. We haven't seen anything in almost an entire day. People die from being stranded in places like this without food or water. When do we reach the point where being free is less important than not dying?

I know the others are thinking it, too, although nobody says it aloud. We're all dragging. Sunburn stings our faces and the backs of our necks. We're not going to get a second wind without at least water. We pass a couple of dried-up ponds, and something that might have once been a creek bed. That's about it. I guess we've picked the wrong time of year for a hike. There isn't so much as a green weed to chew for its moisture.

With the sun still high and blazing, Amber hits the dirt. She doesn't even make a sound; she just wafts to the ground like a slip of paper floating down on an air current.

"We've got to stop," Tori pleads through cracked lips. "Find some shade and lie low until it's not so hot."

"We can't afford the time," Eli argues. "When the Purple People Eaters come after us, we have to be long gone!"

Tori is on her knees. "Amber—wake up!"

Amber is annoyed. "I *am* up. I didn't pass out; I *tripped*."

We look down and that's when we see it—two steel rails on a bed of wooden ties, half buried in dust and weeds.

The train tracks.

We wait forever, but at least we're not walking anymore. I'm pretty sure the track is still in regular use, because the top of the rail is shiny. Still, it's a long, nervous vigil. And the thirst—that's with us every second now. It's like a living thing inside me, a parched sand creature, expanding in size, and royally ticked off.

I pass the time picturing a bottle of water. Seriously,

that's four hours of my life—doing nothing but that.

We notice the vibration first. It's going on for several minutes before we actually hear the train. At last, just as dusk is beginning to settle in, the locomotive appears on the horizon, coming from the west, out of the sunset.

"Why's it going so slow?" Amber wonders.

"It's a freight train," Eli tells her. "And don't complain. We're going to have to jump onto it."

"Why can't we just flag it down?" I ask.

"Because then we'd have to explain who we are and what we're doing here," Eli reasons. "If they start calling around to police stations, asking about runaway kids, the Purples might find out about it."

We retreat from the track and crouch in the brush, sizing up the task ahead of us. One piece of good news— the train is pulling a zillion cars, so we're going to have a very wide selection.

We flatten ourselves to the ground as the engines pass. Once those are out of sight, we approach the track and look for a way in. The liquid tankers are sealed, and the grain hoppers are only accessible from the top.

I point to a flat car stacked with lumber. "One of those?"

Tori shakes her head. "No good. The Purple People Eaters could spot us from their helicopter."

And then a boxcar comes lumbering along, its sliding door open wide. We can see some cargo piled inside, but there's plenty of room.

We look at each other and nod all around. That's the one.

The train may be slow, but when it comes to boarding a moving boxcar, slow is a relative term. We're weak, exhausted, and dehydrated, thanks to twenty-four hours wandering in the wilderness.

There's a long metal step the length of the door opening. Eli hops up on it, but the motion of the train throws off his precarious balance, and he has to jump down again. Amber gets one wobbly foot on it before tumbling back into the dirt. Tori bypasses the step altogether and hurls herself inside. She makes it, but not without whacking one knee on her way in. Now she's pulling away, and the three of us are running beside the track to keep up with her.

"Come *on!*" she wails. I see where she's coming from. The thought of being the only one aboard must be almost as scary as missing the train.

Amber gets there first. Tori reaches out and hauls her aboard. Eli clamps his hands on the side of the doorframe and tries to swing himself inside, but he doesn't have the guts to let go. So he's hanging there at a weird angle, blocking the opening, legs kicking.

"Get inside, stupid!" I pant, running along beside the tracks.

"I can't!"

It's like a scene from a comedy. It would probably be hilarious if our whole lives didn't depend on getting in there.

I give Eli's dangling butt a gigantic push and he goes flying into the car. My toe strikes the edge of a railroad tie, and I start to stumble. I know in my heart, if I fall down, I'll never catch up with the others. My stomach twists at the idea of being left behind.

At the last second, I manage to right myself, hop, skip, and fling my entire body in through the opening.

"Oof!" I hit the floor and roll. I have an awful thought—what if I keep rolling clear out the door on the other side?

Luckily, though, I smack into a heavy pallet of cargo. Something inside gurgles.

I put my fist through the side of the nearest carton and draw out a bottle of blue liquid. I stare at the label. I gawk.

Gatorade!

For the first time in what seems like forever, I smile, and show it to the others.

"Anybody thirsty?"

We have no idea where we're going.

None of us expected to be huddled against crates of Gatorade in a rattling boxcar, so we never bothered to research railway routes or schedules. If things went according to plan, we'd be tooling east in Dad's Lexus. Correction: Felix Hammerstrom's Lexus. He isn't my father anymore. Technically, he never was, any more than the United States was created at a real tea party. He thought he could hide the idea of rebellion from us, and in the end, he got more rebellion than he knew what to do with. Despite the whole-body throb of my wounds, the exhaustion of twenty-four hours on the run, the numbing lack of sleep, the ravenous hunger, and the paralyzing fear over what might lie ahead, I feel a deep satisfaction for that. Project Osiris is officially over.

"Is it?" Amber's not quite so sure. "The whole point of Osiris was to raise us in an ideal environment. Maybe we just lived up to everything our parents expected us to turn into in the first place—the criminal masterminds we're cloned from."

"Masterminds—that's us all right," Malik snorts. "Nobody who saw us getting on the train would accuse us of having any minds at all. Not to mention we screwed up our escape so badly we almost got ourselves killed. And"—his voice drops in volume—"we did get one of us killed."

He reaches for a bottle of Gatorade, but we can see the desolation in his frantic gulping.

"Malik," Tori says gently, "we can't know for sure that Hector didn't make it."

He shakes his head despairingly. "Even if he was with us, we never could have gotten him on the train. He would have wimped out, just like he wimped out of jumping off the truck. It's too bad he won't be around to see us march into Happy Valley with an army of cops!"

Some of the color returns to Amber's pale cheeks. "I'm all for that."

"Let's not get ahead of ourselves," I put in quickly.

"We've got a story to tell, but we'd better be really careful who we tell it to—if we can tell it to anybody at all."

"But we can't do *nothing*," Tori protests. "We owe it to the other clones who are still in Serenity."

"We'll get to that," I promise, "but only when we understand how things work in the real world. Remember, we're clones, and we don't know how that will go over. We're also exact copies of some of the worst criminals in history—younger, but identical. Just because we don't recognize who we're cloned from doesn't mean other people won't."

"We thought we'd have a car," Amber points out. "Without one, we're hiding and hopping trains. We'll never learn enough about the world to figure out how to fit into it."

I pull over a case of bottles and sit down, facing them. "Our best hope is Randy. He knows the outside world but he also knows what it's like to be from Serenity."

"What makes you think we can find him?" Tori asks.

"He's at McNally Academy, outside Pueblo, Colorado. He can give us a place to lie low while we figure out how the world will look at us. It's a boarding school, so we can blend in—no nosy questions about four kids being on their own."

Malik speaks up. "Randy's parents are Osiris researchers. How can we be sure he won't call them and rat us out?"

That's an easy one. "Randy's my best friend," I say with confidence. "He'd never stab me in the back. He'll help us if he can."

I thought I'd never want to walk again, but after a few hours in the boxcar, I'd give anything to stretch my legs. It's the middle of the night now, and we still haven't come to a single town. I'm conjuring a murky vision of the map I saw that time on the plastics factory's internet. I remember that the rail line splits in the eastern part of New Mexico. One branch continues east; the other curls north into Colorado. That's the one we need if we want to end up somewhere near Pueblo. But we won't know which route we've taken until we stop at a station. It's one more variable to sweat over—as if we need another reason to sweat in a hot boxcar.

Malik pulls a fresh case of Gatorade off the pallet, tears it open, and tosses a bottle to each of us. I make no move to catch it, and the container bounces painfully off my face, rolling along the floor of the car. The others share a laugh at my expense, but I barely notice. I'm staring at a sheet of newsprint sticking out of the skid at the base of the pallet. It's from a paper called the *San Bernardino Sun*, and the banner headline blazons:

BARTHOLOMEW GLEN DENIED PAROLE

Something is ringing a bell in my head. But *why?* I've never heard of this guy. How could I? News stories about crime are never allowed to reach kids in Serenity. It's the town's primary mission.

I snatch up the page and begin to read:

Bartholomew Glen, the notorious Crossword Killer, was denied his first petition for parole yesterday. The brilliant but twisted Glen is currently serving nine consecutive life sentences for nine grisly murders. The nickname "Crossword Killer" comes from his habit of taunting the police with clues to his hideous crimes in the form of extremely difficult crossword puzzles. . . .

And then some of the letters in the headline kind of fade out, and I see it as clearly as if it's projected on the wall of the boxcar.

BARTHOLOMEW GLEN
ARTH   OM W G EN

The shock is so total, so horrific, that it's a few moments before I can explain to the others that it's not a direct hit with a Gatorade bottle that has me pale and shaking.

This is the mysterious name on that paper we photographed on the conference table in the factory!

There is only one reason why the name of the Crossword Killer could appear on a document in the very nerve center of Project Osiris: He was one of the criminal masterminds who served as DNA donors for our experiment.

One of us is cloned from Bartholomew Glen.

Our devastation is total. Sure, we knew we were cloned from bad people. But since we never had a name before, I guess we all pictured a cartoonish figure in jail somewhere, maybe even wearing a striped suit. In this vision, the guy— or girl—was a lawbreaker, yes, but also sort of harmless because how much harm can you do from prison?

Bartholomew Glen isn't harmless. He's a psychotic killer with nine innocent people on his conscience. And one of us is an exact copy of him, right down to the last cell.

We pass the paper around, reading and rereading the details of Glen's horrible crimes. We don't want to know, yet somehow, we can't resist.

"When I picture a criminal mastermind," Tori ventures, "it's always a little, you know, romantic. Like an intricately planned scheme to break into the Louvre and steal the *Mona Lisa*. But Bartholomew Glen is just—sick."

"Don't worry," Malik says bitterly. "It can't be either of you. You have to be cloned from his identical twin sister, Bartholomia, the puppy crusher."

"It's not funny, Malik!" Amber exclaims.

"Who's laughing?" Malik retorts. "He's probably me. Toxic element, remember?"

It's a destructive way to think, but now that the cat is out of the bag, we might as well get it out in the open. "There are eleven of us—seven boys and four girls. Bartholomew Glen could be any of the seven. He could even be—" I clam up. It's not going to improve anyone's mood to remember Hector.

"No, not Hector." Malik is adamant. "Hector was a good kid."

"And anyway," I add, "whoever it is didn't kill anybody. This Glen guy did. We have to get used to the idea that we might find out we're cloned from some pretty awful criminals."

We lapse into a melancholy silence, listening to the endless rumble of the train. Amber is the first of us to doze off, a Gatorade bottle clutched in her arms like a newborn baby. Malik is next, falling into troubled dreams. Tori's eyes are closed, but I think she's still awake. Me? No way. Just the idea of Bartholomew Glen and his nine victims is enough to ensure that I may never lay my head down again. I remember Malik's words when I called off the search for Hector—*"At least I'm not stone cold like you."*

Stone cold—if ever there was an expression to describe the Crossword Killer, that's it.

Do I have the strongest reaction to Bartholomew Glen because I'm him?

That turns out to be my last waking thought.

"Eli!"

The voice reaches me through turbulent dreams—exploding trucks lighting up the night; Hector Amani, gone; enemies in purple; Felix Hammerstrom chasing me in his Lexus, the front bumper nudging the backs of my knees as I run for my life. And then I'm down, the weight of the speeding car crunching me like an insect—

"Eli—wake up!"

It's Tori, leaning over and shaking my shoulder. The situation comes hurtling back—the escape, the train, the lifesaving Gatorade. Malik and Amber are just rousing from sleep. The train—never very fast—is slowing down. It's just after dawn, the sun still low in the sky. Through the open door of the boxcar, we can see signs of civilization—buildings, houses, power lines, roads.

"Is this a city?" Amber whispers.

"I don't think so," Malik replies. "But it's bigger than anything we're used to. Crummier too."

He's right. Some of the houses along the tracks are really ramshackle, and the fencing is torn and rusty. In Serenity, nothing is ever allowed to stay broken or even unpainted. That doesn't seem to be the case out here.

We roll past a faded sign: *Colorado City.*

"Colorado!" I breathe, encouraged that we've come north. I have no clue where Pueblo is, but at least we're not heading east, away from McNally Academy and Randy.

Brakes screech as the train lurches to a stop in the middle of a rail yard. Stacks of lumber and pieces of equipment are scattered all around. Skids loaded with cargo are lined up along the track beside several forklift trucks.

"What's that stuff for?" Amber wonders.

The answer comes all too soon. A yard worker in coveralls and a hard hat leaps in the door of the boxcar, turning to signal an approaching forklift. He takes one look at the four of us and barks, "What are you kids doing here?"

Since we have no answer for that, the only course of action is flight. Tori is the first to react. She runs for the open door, which is suddenly blocked by a huge pallet of cargo carried by forklift arms.

The worker puts an iron grip on her wrist. With his free hand, he grabs a walkie-talkie from his belt. "Security to car thirty-six!"

Amber and I watch in horror, but Malik springs into battle. He snatches up a full Gatorade bottle and bounces it with deadly accuracy off the side of the man's jaw. The blow knocks him backward into the wall, and he releases Tori. The four of us make a break for freedom. With the doorway blocked by cargo, Tori squeezes through the gap to the right of the incoming load; Amber and I slip out the opening on the left. The worker reaches for Malik, who drops to the floor and tries to roll under the arms of the forklift.

He almost makes it. The pallet descends and he's trapped beneath it, screaming for help.

Tori and I reach in and try to pull him out, but his legs are stuck as the wooden skid slowly comes down. In a matter of seconds, he'll be squashed.

Amber doesn't hesitate. She leaps into the cab of the forklift, dislodging the driver. The man is so shocked at being suddenly and aggressively attacked by a thirteen-year-old girl that he topples out the other side and sprawls onto the gravel. She slams the heel of her hand into the control and pushes it in the opposite direction. The load lifts off Malik and rises, striking the boxcar's ceiling. Malik scrambles free, Amber jumps down, and the four of us take off.

A pudgy uniformed security guard is running along the track in our direction. We look around desperately.

"There!" Tori exclaims, pointing to some trees.

There's a tall chain-link fence in the way, but luckily, the mesh has torn away from the post. We slither underneath and sprint for the woods. It's the last thing any of us need in our starved and exhausted state. Yet at this point in our adventure, capture is not an option. If we're arrested here, the local police will start looking for our parents. Then it's only a matter of time before we're in the custody of the Purple People Eaters.

I risk a look back and see the security man helping the two workers bring the forklift's payload down from the boxcar's ceiling. I guess railway business is more important than four stowaway kids. But as soon as the cargo is where it's supposed to be, they might come after us again. We have to act fast.

Abruptly, the woods come to an end, and we blunder onto a busy street. Tires squeal and a big SUV lurches to a halt six inches from my chest. The driver leaps out from behind the wheel, white-faced. "Are you kids okay?"

"Sorry!" I blurt, and we hustle back onto the sidewalk. We've only been in this town a few minutes and already we've been caught, chased, and almost run over. Has our Serenity upbringing left us so clueless that we're doomed to blunder from near miss to near miss? How long before one of those close calls turns into a real disaster?

Right now, the odds of us making it in the outside world seem like a million to one.

The sights and sounds are overwhelming—car horns and the faces of so many people we don't know. The road is filled with more vehicles than we've ever seen all in one place.

I struggle to make sense of where I am. It's not a big city, but both sides of the road are lined with stores and restaurants, and people are coming and going. This must be the downtown.

My eyes fall on an older car parked at the curb. It's painted yellow with a black-and-white checker pattern and a driver sitting inside. Something about it looks familiar but I can't quite put my finger on it.

Tori follows my gaze. "Is that a taxi?"

Of course! There are no taxis in Serenity, where an eight-minute walk would take you across town. But from books I've read and movies I've seen, taxis will drive you wherever you want to go. Like away from the train depot, for example. Or to McNally Academy.

We run for the car and pile into the backseat. "We have to go to Pueblo," I tell the driver.

She peers at the four of us in the rearview mirror. "That's an hour's trip. Are you sure you kids can afford the ride?"

We begin digging in our pockets for the money we've been hoarding. It's a nerve-racking moment, since we have very little sense of what things cost beyond the borders of our hometown. We produce our stash, fistfuls of crumpled bills, wadded up and spotted with dirt and blood. It would buy a lot at our general store, but everything in Serenity is so artificial that our life experience is basically worthless. Plus none of us has ever been in a taxi before, much less paid for one. For all we know, it's the most expensive thing you can do. We can't predict whether our money will be enough to take us to Pueblo, or even down the block.

Our driver opens wide eyes at the sight of our bills—ones, fives, tens, twenties, fifties, hundreds. "For that," she laughs, "I can take you to Bangor, Maine."

"Just Pueblo, please," I say politely.

For the first time, she turns around and looks at us over the seat. She sees what we've gotten used to: We are sunburned, scratched, bruised, disheveled, and filthy, not to mention red-eyed and exhausted. "What happened to you kids? Maybe we should stop at a hospital first!"

"No hospital!" I exclaim urgently. "We have to get to Pueblo—to McNally Academy!"

She stares at me for a moment, and then starts the car. "You rich private school kids!" she snorts. "The shenanigans you get into while you're spending Daddy's money.

You're going to be in big trouble when the teachers get a look at you!"

"Probably," Tori agrees solemnly.

The taxi pulls away from the curb.

We've passed our first real-world test.

Pueblo looks run-down and neglected compared to Serenity, but the red-tile-roofed adobe brick buildings of McNally Academy are the nicest things we've seen so far. The campus is in the hill country a few miles outside of town, nestled among the high-desert pines.

The taxi leaves us, two hundred dollars poorer, on the school's main drive. It's chillier than Serenity, still morning. Students are everywhere, on their way to breakfast and morning classes.

"Whoa," Amber whispers. "Did you ever think there were this many kids in the whole world?"

There are maybe a hundred of them scattered around. But when you're used to a place where there are only thirty—and zero unfamiliar faces—this counts as a mob scene.

"Get used to it," Malik comments. "That's one thing they've got plenty of in the outside world—people."

"We're only interested in one person," I remind them. I notice that we're starting to attract attention, and not just because we're scratched and beaten up and our clothes are torn and dirty. McNally may seem crowded to us, but it's probably not a huge school. Chances are, the students all know each other, so newcomers stand out. If any teachers see us, they're going to ask questions. "Let's find Randy before the adults who run this place want to know what we're doing here."

Still, we hang back. We don't talk to strangers; in Serenity, there *are* no strangers, if you don't count the Purple People Eaters. How would you approach someone you've never met before? The McNally kids are all in groups, chatting amiably. The fact that they *belong* only emphasizes the reality that we don't.

Malik is the first one to work up the guts. He targets a boy around our age walking alone. "Hey," he calls, "you know a guy named Randy Hardaway?"

The boy stops and looks us over. "Yeah, I know Randy." He obviously notices that we're a mess but decides not to ask about it. "Are you friends of his?"

I nod. "From his hometown. Can you point us to him?"

"This is kind of a surprise visit," adds Tori.

320

"He's probably in his dorm room—Hayden thirty-three," the kid tells us. "Randy skips breakfast and sleeps till five minutes before class. He's kind of famous for it."

I can't help smiling. Some things never change.

He points out the right building and we hurry in that direction. The sign reads:

HAYDEN CENTER FOR STUDENT LIVING
BOYS ONLY

It doesn't seem to be a hard-and-fast rule, though. There are both boys and girls in the hall, milling around, calling for each other, shoving books into backpacks, and generally gearing up for a day of classes. A nervous glance flashes among the four of us. The hallway is crowded. At close range, under indoor lighting, our bedraggled state and our *otherness* will be even more painfully obvious.

At first, we just stand there, helpless. The corridor is wall-to-wall people, and moving through a crowd is something we have no experience with. It's Malik who finally figures it out, mostly because he's big enough to clear a path. The rest of us get behind him and follow in his wake.

The McNally kids stare at us as we pass, some of them

from mere inches away. A low murmur goes up in the hall. Who are we? Why are we here? An eerie dread takes hold of me and I begin to shiver in spite of the heat of my sunburned skin. In my mind, I'm thinking: *This is what it's like to be a clone in the real world—a strange curiosity, not quite human, not quite acceptable, possibly dangerous.*

I tell myself no one could know that. We're the focal point because we're battered, ragged strangers, not because of the invisible history of our birth. But I can't escape a deep foreboding that people will be looking at us for those other reasons soon enough.

Malik stops dead, and the three of us bump into him from behind.

"Here it is," he tells me. "Room thirty-three."

He steps aside and I knock. The report of my knuckles on the wooden door echoes inside my head, reverberating from temple to temple. The kids in the hall gather around like this is the eighteenth hole of a championship golf tournament.

For the first few seconds, nothing happens. The silence is so total that it's almost as if these McNally kids realize that what they're witnessing is the most important moment in our lives.

There's a scrambling sound inside the room. The